Praise for *PARADISE RULES*

■

"Wickedly funny. Ballsy and bold. An authentic adolescent narrator who you can't help but love. I found myself thinking about Gates long after I finished the book. I think this will be Gleacher's breakthrough book."

—James Frey, *New York Times* bestselling author
of *Bright Shiny Morning*

"Hilarious, disturbing, and stylish. Gleacher writes about the untapped subject of the gray area created when a teenage boy and an older woman enter a sexual relationship. Gleacher writes about this taboo sexuality in an adventurous fashion through a seventeen-year-old narrator who bursts with heart even during his most mischievous moments."

—Pittacus Lore, *New York Times* bestselling author
of *I Am Number Four*

"Sex, golf and gambling. Friendship, family and love. Gleacher exposes the sordid underbelly of these unholy trinities with great humor, rollicking exuberance, and a massive abundance of heart."

—David Goodwillie, author of the *New York Times* Notable Book *American Subversive*

"Alternately sweet and dark, exploring an older woman's sexual relationship with a teenage boy. We see the opposite all too often and Gleacher's take is unique, navigating all the confusion and destruction, yet there is humor woven into every beautiful page."

—Jill Kargman, national bestselling author of *Sometimes I Feel Like a Nut*

"One of the funniest and most provocative coming-of-age novels I've ever read. Once again Jimmy Gleacher has managed to be simultaneously heartbreaking and hilarious."

—Carrie Karasyov, national bestselling author of *The Infidelity Pact*

Paradise Rules is also available as an eBook

paradise *rules*

jimmy gleacher

GALLERY BOOKS

New York London Toronto Sydney

Gallery Books
A Division of Simon & Schuster, Inc.
1230 Avenue of the Americas
New York, NY 10020

First Gallery Books trade paperback edition July 2011

GALLERY BOOKS and colophon are trademarks of Simon & Schuster, Inc.

For information about special discounts for bulk purchases, please contact Simon & Schuster Special Sales at 1-866-506-1949 or business@ simonandschuster.com.

The Simon & Schuster Speakers Bureau can bring authors to your live event. For more information or to book an event contact the Simon & Schuster Speakers Bureau at 1-866-248-3049 or visit our website at www .simonspeakers.com.

Designed by Jaime Putorti

Manufactured in the United States of America

10 9 8 7 6 5 4 3 2 1

Library of Congress Cataloging-in-Publication Data is available.

ISBN 978-1-4516-0845-8
ISBN 978-1-4516-0882-3 (ebook)

For my dad, who inspires me with his hard work, makes me proud with his success and philanthropy, and pisses me off on the golf course with his unsolicited advice. He is a man who can wear Phat Farm, Lululemon, and Loro Piana all in the same outfit. He can explain the intricacies of investment banking or recite every single one of Samuel L. Jackson's lines from *Pulp Fiction*. He talks to doormen with the same respect as he does a CEO. He is a self-made man of the people, but he is only a father to six, and I am lucky to be one of them.

acknowledgments

Thanks to my agent Alex Glass, and all his colleagues at Trident Media Group. Thanks to my editor Megan McKeever, and to everyone at Gallery Books who worked on *Paradise Rules*. Thanks to John Paul Jones at Simon & Schuster for his copyedits. Thanks to Sean Carr for his help with development and revisions. Thanks to Jim Margulis and Amy Benton for their feedback on rough drafts. Thanks to Ed Herlihy for being one of my greatest supporters. Thanks to Little Mikey for his songs about Robin. And thanks to You, for reading my book. It was a privilege to have you as an audience.

Rest in peace Bernie Rogers. Tony, Vandy, and everyone else you touched misses you daily.

paradise *rules*

paradise rules

i wish I could say I was a victim but I willingly played into the devil's hands. My reasons weren't always right and my justifications weren't just, but my weaknesses were common. My name is Gates and I've been sexually deviant since the day I hit puberty. In the last week I almost killed one man and swindled a fortune from another but those are not my greatest sins. I'm seventeen years old and I may have just ruined my life.

I go to public school here in Boulder, Colorado, and just finished junior year. Everyone calls me Casper because I never hang out but people like me so I'm considered a friendly ghost. Nicknames are cool unless they're stupid like mine. I also caddy at a country club and my nickname there is Fun Buns. Being a teenager can be a bitch like that

jimmy gleacher

but I've had it pretty easy. I don't really look funny and I play a varsity sport so all I really need to do is keep my head down and do my time until I can go away to college.

I have two best friends. A girl named Melanie and a guy named Timmy Timmy Timmy. Timmy Timmy Timmy's real name is just Timmy but his OCD makes him repeat the final word of every sentence three times so everyone calls him Timmy Timmy Timmy or 3T's for short. Most kids would probably want to chug a bottle of drain cleaner if they had the same affliction but Timmy Timmy Timmy's the best looking guy to have ever walked the halls of Boulder High. He's literally a model and half the time he isn't even in school because he's working in New York or Los Angeles or Miami or anywhere else they need someone good-looking. He makes more money than our principal.

Not many kids want to hang out with Timmy Timmy Timmy. Speech impediments and high school go together like explosive diarrhea and international plane flights. But every month 3T's picture is either in a fashion magazine or on the cover of a clothing catalogue so no one ever messes with him because if they did he'd steal their girlfriend faster than they could say Abercrombie & Fitch Fitch Fitch.

My other best friend is Melanie Vanleer and she's the reason I'm sitting here today writing this all down. Until a few days ago Mel and I were a couple and for a while everything was perfect until she wanted to have sex. She's two

2

inches taller than me and can hit her driver two hundred and fifty yards. She's a jock but not a tomboy because she likes to wear dresses and paint her nails. We started hanging out the spring of our sophomore year when we both made the varsity golf team. I was the number one player and she was the number five player, on the boy's team. Some of the older guys kinda hated us for that so they ostracized us but we were outcasts by then anyway. She was an oversized jock in a world where girls were sticking toothbrushes down their throats to stay undersized and I was the loner who missed an entire year of school because his mom Chernobyled and got shipped off to the loony bin. But we had golf and the game was as much a diversion for Mel as it was for me and in each other we found a partner for our escape.

At first we didn't kiss or flirt or even flirt with flirting but then I fell for her. She'd never be a cheerleader and she'd always be big boned but she was a beautiful athletic girl and more importantly had a soul worth loving. All the other girls in our school, even the smart and nice ones, still seemed like a work in progress while Mel carried herself like a finished product. There's probably five hundred places I could start this story but I'll begin from only twelve days ago when Mel and I were playing golf and she hit her ball in a sand trap. Mel was wearing a periwinkle skirt and a white sleeveless top and her arms and legs were already tan. Her shiny black hair was tied into pigtails with periwinkle ribbons. Periwinkle made her blue eyes brighter so she wore the color often. Mel was no dummy. When we got to the bunker we found her ball in a deep footprint that someone should have raked. Mel laughed at her bad luck when a lot of other people would have cussed. I picked up her ball, smoothed out the footprint and carefully placed it back in the original spot.

Mel said, "Um . . . I may not be the high school state champion for the third consecutive year but I'm pretty sure that's a no-no."

"Paradise Rules, baby."

"Baby?" She laughed. "That's pretty racy talk for such a prude. What the hell is Paradise Rules?"

"Paradise Rules. If you don't like your lie you can fix it with no penalty."

"Oh, you mean cheating." Mel picked up her ball and dug her foot into the sand to make a new, deeper print and then put the ball back. I loved her for doing that. She opened up the face of her wedge and swung straight down at the ball and it popped onto the green and rolled right past the hole. It was a good shot and I loved her for that too. I loved her for calling me Prude and for wearing periwinkle and for using the word hell. I loved her for everything that made her who she was.

We walked up on the green and Mel squatted behind

her ball and tried to determine which direction the grain would break her putt. She made a good roll at it but missed the cup on the low side by a couple of inches and she shook her head as she flipped the ball up with the back of her putter and caught it in midair. Something came over me and I blurted out, "You don't know me, Mel. Not the real me."

"I don't?" Mel held the flagstick a few feet from the cup and casually stood with a hand on her hip and one foot crossed behind her ankle. I placed my ball on my mark and my hand was shaking but Mel didn't notice because she was staring west at a long horizontal cloud covering the foothills nearby. She smiled but wanted me to putt so we could move on to the next hole. The girl loved to play fast and I loved her for that. She glanced at my ball as a signal for me to hurry up and wasn't taking my attempted confession seriously.

I relaxed, sank the putt and we started walking to the next tee but Mel stopped short and turned on her heels and grabbed the front of my shirt. "You got three seconds to say whatever the hell it is you're trying to tell me."

I tried to make her let go but she was really strong. "Jesus, Mel. Calm down."

"The fuck I will. You've been beating around the bush for the past three months that you want to tell me something, so tell me." She caught me completely off guard and that had been her plan, playing it cool on the green with her hand on her hip as she stared into space all the while waiting to pounce. She'd make a great hustler, another reason to love her. All I was getting was reason after reason after reason to love her so I decided if she gave me one more reason I would tell her the whole sordid truth.

"It's nothing, alright?"

"Pussy," she said, and let me go. And that was the last reason I needed to love her: my girlfriend called me a pussy.

So I had to tell her, I wanted to tell her, I'd been dying to tell her but it didn't seem realistic to tap her on the shoulder and just lay it all out. So I guess that's what this story is all about: how I was finally able to spill my rotten guts.

We finished the round in peace and I got on my bike and rode to Harmony's Rest, a retirement home where I read to senior citizens. Phyllis, the woman who gave me the volunteer job, was waiting with a copy of Kate Chopin's *The Awakening*. She was seventy-five and not too many years away from living in the home herself but she was pissed at me and any woman who's angry, young or old, is a force to be reckoned with.

Phyllis greeted me with a scowl and a pointed finger. "What made you think you could read them a book about the mafia and I wouldn't find out? These people are fragile.

You can't fill their heads with hit men and pistols. Mrs. Green woke up the entire floor screaming in the middle of the night because she thought a man named Carlo was trying to lock her in the trunk of his car." She crossed her arms, lowered her chin and stared me down, but then in a friendlier tone added, "If you're not going to follow my rules, this won't work."

I felt badly about Mrs. Green but everyone hated *The Awakening* and asked me to sneak in "racier" material. "Can I at least read them something from this century?"

Phyllis handed me *The Awakening* and said, "My way or the highway . . . Carlo."

I headed to the dining hall where an elderly group eagerly awaited the finale of *Mob Slob*, a shoot-'em-up comedy about the bumbling son (Carlo) of a mafia kingpin who botched hits on purpose because he didn't want to murder anyone. We had one chapter left and the crowd wanted to know if Carlo was gonna flip to the feds but instead they got *The Awakening*.

After a few pages everyone was asleep except for an old blind man named Cliff who wore big black boxy sunglasses that hid half his face. Cliff always sat right next to me and we were pals. He covered his ears and said, "Stop! What happened to Carlo?"

"The gig is up, Cliff."

He grimaced. "It was Greeny, wasn't it? I knew she was

a weak link." One thing about retirement homes, the people move slowly but the gossip doesn't. "Bring in something saucy tomorrow. I'll handle Greeny."

I looked around the room. Two of the napping seniors had drool dripping down their chins. "I can't, Cliff. I promised Phyllis I wouldn't."

Cliff patted my knee and said, "There's no honor in honesty if it's destructive."

I thought about my relationship with Mel and said, "That's what I've been telling myself for the past two years."

Cliff growled, "Mmm, I wish you wouldn't make comments like that."

"I know, but I gotta be honest with somebody."

I left the sleepy group of seniors and rode my bike back to the golf course. The Boulder Golf Club is a private membership where I worked as a caddy and through a special arrangement with the owner, Lu, was allowed to play and practice. None of the other caddies were permitted to use the facilities. Lu told them I was special because I was a scratch golfer and won the state tourney three years in a row but he didn't really care about any of that. Lu only cared about one thing: money.

When I got to the course I decided to work on my putting and soon enough Lu and a fellow caddy and teammate named Wade came to watch. Wade was in my class and had a side business selling drugs. He was tall and wiry and had a mop of blond hair and his eyes were always hidden beneath a visor he wore low over his face. He was the kind of kid that mothers didn't want their sons hanging out with. Wade's parents are former celebrities. His dad is Ike Peterson, the bassist for Goner, a popular eighties band whose songs still play on the radio. Wade's mom is Sara Peters, a B actress from that same decade who was famous in a cult kind of way because she played Hope Woebegone in the slasher flicks *Dead Duck, Dead Duck 2* and *Dead Duck 3*. *Dead Duck* was about a duck-hunting retreat where hunters visited and were never seen again. It was so bad it was good and so they made three, each one worse and thus better than the next. There were pictures of Sara Peters nude on the internet. The photos were from the eighties. In one she sunbathed nude in front of a pool boy who wore a white uniform and licked a dripping ice-cream cone. In another she wore fingerless gloves and fishnets on her arms and had such a huge bush between her legs it was hard to tell where her crotch ended and her thighs began. The joke on Wade was to crowbar the word *hair* into every conversation with him.

Lu was a short, plump Chinese man in his fifties who dressed like a teenage Beverly Hills prepster in pastel-colored shirts with starched collars. Whenever Lu got nervous he'd say phony Confucius quotes in an exaggerated

Chinese accent like, "Man who go through airport turnstile sideways going to Bangkok." Converting the BGC from a public course into a private club was his idea. He hired Rees Jones, the world's greatest golf course architect, to re-design the course and he renovated the clubhouse. After all the improvements there still weren't many members though, so the place was hurting for cash.

Wade and Lu made quite a pair. Wade was half a foot taller than Lu and looked like a scarecrow in his baggy clothes and stringy hair. Lu wore a bright pink shirt that was too tight and pushed out by his belly. He looked like an Easter egg. They were standing on the fringe of the green in front of the cup I was aimed at. My first ball went in, then my second, and before I hit my third I asked, "How much you guys got on this?"

"A hundy," Wade answered.

"Who bet against me?"

Wade raised his hand and said, "Whodaya think, Fun Buns?"

"What if I only miss by a hair?"

"I don't know. What if your girlfriend wasn't built like a linebacker, then no one would think you're gay."

"I'm just saying it's kind of a hairy putt." I pointed at the grass in front of me and said, "That break is like a hair-pin turn."

"Just hit it already, Fun Buns."

I made the putt and Wade handed over his money to Lu and stormed off. Once we were alone Lu said, "Got a game for you tomorrow."

I shook my head. "Sorry but I'm out."

"You're out?" He laughed. "You're not out, there is no out. Besides, I thought you liked our agreement."

"I do. But . . ."

"There's nothing to feel guilty about."

"Sure there is."

Lu was wearing red, white and blue boating shoes. He looked at them a minute and then asked, "What about boarding school? How you gonna pay for tuition if you jump off the gravy train?"

"There's other ways to make money."

Lu punched my arm playfully and said, "Lighten up, Chawlie." He thought a moment and said, "You want some advice? Because I'll give you some real advice if you promise to listen."

He sounded sincere so I replied. "Please."

Lu switched to his Confucius voice and said, "Panties not best thing on earth, but next to best thing on earth," and walked away.

I went straight from the BGC to the library and studied until it closed. Then I had to go home. I thought about crashing at Harmony's Rest but I was starving and wanted food. I didn't like going home because my godmother

Alicia lived with us. She's a child psychologist and Mom's security blanket. She moved in two years ago after Mom had a nervous breakdown and tried to kill herself. Alicia checked Mom into a "hospital" in Arizona for nine months and took me out of school so we could live full-time at her weekend house in Aspen. When Mom finally made it back to Boulder it had been decided Alicia would move in with us. She had her own bedroom and set of keys and she spent more time in the house than Mom who buried herself in her real estate company. Mom was a stunningly beautiful woman and I guess a lot of people out there think a pretty face can sell a house because she had listings throughout Denver and Boulder and her smiling face beamed from FOR SALE signs planted in front yards everywhere. Sometimes it felt like I could never escape her but that's what a guilty conscience will do.

When I got home from the library Alicia's BMW was in the driveway where it always was. The woman never went out. She was never married, had no children and didn't once have a serious boyfriend. One time I asked Mom why this was and she replied, "Because maybe that's how she wants it." Alicia could get a guy if she wanted. She's no centerfold but she's not a troll either. She's got big fake boobs that are totally hypnotic but when she goes out in public she dresses like a nun and doesn't put on any makeup or do anything to try and look good. Most women do all kinds of crap to get a man to notice them but Alicia did the opposite.

When I walked in the house I wanted to sneak into the kitchen and grab something to eat but Alicia was sitting in the living room facing the front door reading one of her shrink magazines and drinking a glass of red wine. She smiled and said, "He's home." Alicia had really high cheekbones that made her look like a chipmunk and when she smiled her eyes pretty much disappeared. I waved and headed for the stairs but she called out, "Not so fast," and hopped out of her chair. She was wearing a slinky blue silk camisole and a short white miniskirt, clothes she only wore around the house. "I made dinner if you're hungry."

"Thanks. I'm good. Where's Mom?"

"She's entertaining a client in Denver and is staying down there. Probably because she doesn't want to drive back too late."

"Too late, or too drunk?"

Alicia gave me a disapproving look and crossed her arms beneath her boobs, which made them stick out even more. "Don't be so hard on her."

"I like it better when she's here," I said.

"So do I." She frowned and added, "But at least we have the house to ourselves."

I tried not to look at her or stare at her tits and fall under their spell. She was a voluptuous woman and even though she had a few extra pounds they were in all the right places. About a month ago Wade dropped me off after a golf match and he came in to use the bathroom. Alicia thought I was alone and sauntered down the stairs wearing nothing but a towel on her head and white lingerie. She was fresh out of the shower and pretended to be looking for the iron. When Wade came out of the bathroom they both froze and then Alicia sprinted up the stairs.

Wade and I watched her run all the way to her room and then he turned to me and said, "Dude . . ."

"My godmother," I explained

He nodded and remarked, "G-MILF."

The next day at school Wade came up to me and said, "I thought about your godmother last night when I was holding my sausage hostage. She's the new star of my spank bank." This became his running joke and in front of the entire golf team including Melanie he'd talk about how Alicia had a butter-face but that he'd still like to "titty-bang her until her implants popped." This went on and on until I stole a pair of Alicia's underwear, covered them with itching powder and put them in a Ziploc bag and gave them to Wade. I told him Alicia had a crush on him and he was cocky enough to believe it. That night he sent me a text message that said UR DEAD! Wade's dick burned so bad his mom had to drive him to the emergency room. The next day he brought me a pair of his dad's boxers and said, "I thought you'd get off on these since you only date boys." He was at least nice enough not to say it in front of Mel. That was the thing about Wade, he was a prick but he had flashes of decency. Growing up with Mom taught me how to soak in people's briefest glimpses of good so I actually liked Wade more than most people did.

Alicia walked toward me so I headed up the stairs before she could get too close. When I got to my room I reached under my bed to grab a Tupperware container where I stashed peanut butter, bread, bottled water and potato chips for nights just like this one but it was gone. Alicia opened my door without knocking and said, "If you're looking for your food it's in the kitchen."

I went to bed hungry and thought about Melanie and her periwinkle ribbons, how she liked to call me Prude and the way she grabbed my shirt; but the thing I thought about most was her footprint in the sand.

the worst kind of criminal

*t*he next morning I crept down to the kitchen and found my container with the food and water sitting on the counter. I grabbed a Coke from the fridge and made a peanut butter and potato chip sandwich and devoured them both in thirty seconds then belted out a burp that bounced through the house. It was six-thirty, the sun had risen and a squirrel and magpie were chasing each other up and down a tree in the yard. They did this every morning and I could never tell if they were fighting, playing or flirting. It didn't seem natural to have a bird and a squirrel so wrapped up in each other's lives but this was their routine and it seemed like on some level they needed each other.

During the nine months Mom was in the "hospital" Alicia remodeled our home as a surprise gift. Mom had lived in the house for fifteen years; she bought it when she was pregnant with me, and Alicia said it was full of bad memories. The house originally had four small bedrooms upstairs and a kitchen, living room, den and a dining room downstairs. Alicia opened up the living room and kitchen into one big space and the dining room and den that overlooked the backyard were converted into a master bedroom for Mom, complete with a marble bathroom and steam shower. Hardwood floors were installed throughout the main level; plush carpeting ran wall to wall upstairs. She also knocked down the bedroom walls, turning four small rooms into two, and replaced my bunk beds with a queen.

Alicia was always doing nice things for Mom but Mom never reciprocated because she constantly fluctuated between love and hate for Alicia. Alicia said Mom had a borderline personality disorder so I looked up the illness online and it was like reading a perfect description of Mom. I guess there's a reason Alicia's such a successful psychologist. People literally wait four months just to see her. She charges more than any other shrink in Colorado. Magazines write articles about her. Lawyers pay for her analysis. She even did some consulting for the FBI.

Mom was always embroiled in some kind of drama, be it with a fellow Realtor, a mortgage broker or a house inspector, but if things were fine at work she'd stir things up with Alicia. They'd get drunk or high and fight all night. In the morning I'd find Alicia passed out on the living room couch and china smashed in the kitchen. Then I'd head off to school knowing that when I got home Alicia would be waiting for me.

Shortly following my burp Alicia walked into the kitchen and said, "What did you swallow? A cannon?" She was wearing a faded blue oxford shirt that was frayed at the cuffs and the collar. It was a big shirt that hung below her waist and even though she never wore anything beneath it she usually secured the bottom few buttons to cover herself. But that morning I was treated to a full view of her landing strip. This was nothing I hadn't seen before. When we lived in Aspen Alicia often roamed the house in her underwear or completely nude. She stopped when we moved back to Boulder and at first I kind of missed it, which totally made me hate myself even more. But then whenever she and Mom got in a fight her clothes came off and she'd come looking for me. Sometimes I'd hide, sometimes I wouldn't. When I started to fall for Mel I bought a deadbolt for my bedroom door but Mom made me take it down. She thought I got it to do drugs in my room. I should have told Mom everything then but didn't want her to slit her wrists again. And, I guess if I'm really truly being honest, part of me didn't want things to end with Alicia. She was the only person in the world who gave me affection; having sex with her was a price I was willing to pay.

Alicia took the bag of potato chips out of my hand and said, "No junk food for breakfast."

"You're flashing your snatch Alicia. My breakfast should be the last fucking thing on your mind."

Alicia quickly buttoned her shirt. "Don't be ridiculous. And don't use that word."

"Which word? *Snatch, fuck* or *breakfast*?"

Mom's white convertible pulled into the driveway and Alicia rolled the bag of chips shut and handed it to me and said, "Breakfast, shithead," before running upstairs.

A minute later Mom walked in the door. She had a boyfriend who lived on our street but she didn't want anyone to know about him. She'd even hide her car in his garage but I busted her leaving his house at 4 A.M. during spring break when I was sneaking back home from a party at Wade's. I didn't know why Mom wanted to keep him a secret; he seemed like a nice guy and he wore a tie to work and everything. Alicia figured it out three months ago and that's when things got really bad again.

Mom tossed her purse on the counter and said, "You're up early."

"This is when I always get up."

"I thought teenagers were supposed to sleep until noon."

"They are."

"Hey, remember that house in Denver I sold a few

months ago? The really big one with the bowling alley and the indoor swimming pool? We closed last night. My biggest sale ever." She was so happy and proud and I was proud of her too so I dropped the attitude and gave her a high-five.

"Was J'Marcus there?" I asked. J'Marcus Cadillac was this year's Heisman Trophy winner and the Denver Broncos' first-round draft pick. He's also Mom's client.

"Yup. He flew in with his agent and his grandmother, signed the papers and then we went out to dinner to celebrate and I drank so much champagne I got a hotel room! Ha! But I deserved it. That reminds me . . ." She ran out to her car.

A few seconds later Alicia resurfaced wearing sweats and a baggy T-shirt. I said, "Nice pj's," and offered her a potato chip.

Mom walked back into the kitchen and threw me a football signed by J'Marcus. "Gotcha a closing bonus."

Alicia shouted, "You closed!" and she and Mom shrieked like eighth graders and threw their arms around each other. Alicia slid her hands to the small of Mom's back and Mom did the same to her, which pressed their hips together. Mom beamed and said, "Sometimes I just can't believe how lucky we are." Her eyes were so unconvinced of her words she needed me to concur so I nodded and smiled and hopped off my seat and headed for the door while Mom and Alicia stayed locked in their embrace.

We were in the middle of exam week but I didn't have any tests that day so I went to the golf course and brought Lu the autographed ball hoping it might butter him up a little. He was alone in the pro shop reading the paper and I tossed him the pigskin, which he clumsily caught with both hands. "What the hell is this?" he asked, trying to read the signature.

"It's J'Marcus Cadillac's autograph."

"It is?" Lu studied J'Marcus's scribble. "Did he sign this during an earthquake or something?"

"I dunno. Have you ever tried to sign a football? It's probably not that easy."

Lu looked at the ball again. "That's right, your mom sold him his house. There's a picture of them in the paper today. That's a serious pad."

"Yeah, Mom was pretty psyched. I guess they went out to dinner afterward and Mom got so tanked she had to get a hotel room." I didn't know why I was talking so much, probably because I was nervous. "That's for you," I said pointing at the ball.

Lu looked at me dubiously. "For me?"

"As a thanks. For letting me play here."

He threw back the ball. "You know why I let you play here."

"But I told you last night I'm done."

"And I'm telling you today. You're playing." Lu wore a white cable-knit sweater over a white collared shirt and white pants. "Quit tomorrow if you must but I got a game for you right now and these cats are fat."

I scratched my head a moment and asked, "Are you trying to sound cool or uncool?"

"I'm trying to help you run away to boarding school like you always talk about."

Lu was a goofy guy but every once in a while he could be pretty intimidating. I still had to ask, "Why are you dressed for Wimbledon?"

Lu lifted up the front page of the newspaper and pointed at a picture of Mom and J'Marcus standing in J'Marcus's new cobblestone driveway. He read the caption beneath the photograph: "J'Marcus Cadillac flew into Denver on a private jet yesterday morning to show his grandmother their new house and sign ownership papers before boarding the jet two hours later and returning home to Houston. Cadillac says he plans to move to Denver full-time before mini-camp starts in July." Lu folded down the paper and said, "See, everybody lies. Even your mother."

"You're an asshole."

Lu put on his Chinaman voice and replied, "Man who live in glass house should change clothes in basement."

When Lu redesigned the BGC and made the club private there weren't a lot of members at first so he made a deal with the fanciest hotel in town that allowed their guests to pay a greens fee and play the course. A hundred and seventy-five bucks bought eighteen holes plus a cart and it wasn't unusual for there to be more hotel customers on the course than club members. A lot of the visitors were businessmen playing on the tab of their corporate accounts and Lu greased a concierge at the hotel to tell him which ones were high rollers. My job was to play these men in golf and take all their money and in return I was granted unlimited access to the BGC and half my winnings.

That day I was paired with three men from Omaha who were fat, rich and happy. I guess money doesn't buy fashion sense because their shirts were kaleidoscopes of silver, mauve, turquoise and bronze and they wore black socks with shorts. They hucked instead of laughed and constantly talked about a guy they worked for, named Warren. They were decent enough players and had bets on just about every shot—longest drive, closest to the pin, and birdies were all worth twenty bucks. They loved money, they loved talking about money and most of all they loved taking each other's money. They also loved saying their boss's name.

The men didn't seem too keen on my joining them and when I snap-hooked my drive off the first tee into the trees one of them groaned. My second shot ricocheted off a tree and bounced the wrong way down the fairway. I topped my third shot, skulled my fourth and hit my fifth in a bunker and picked up. On the second tee I was invisible. The men exchanged bills tallying who owed who what and then hit and began walking off the tee before remembering I was there. They apologized and got out of the way and then watched me hit a huge slice into a pond. I dropped at the hazard, nuked my second shot over the green, chipped it short, two-putted and walked to the next tee with my head down. The men were already there and one of them was saying, "Warren told me the best pancakes he ever had was in Minneapolis."

A different guy scraped a tee beneath his fingernails and said, "That right? He told me always order oatmeal in Columbus, doesn't matter which diner, the good oatmeal is citywide."

"Did he tell you where to fix a slice?" I asked.

The man cleaning his nails said, "Nope. But Warren always says, 'If you want results . . . get invested.'"

The third man asked, "How much money you carrying, son?"

I pulled out my wallet and counted forty-two dollars. The men watched me sort through the crumpled bills and I said, "This'll last one hole the way you guys are going."

The second man finished cleaning his nails and examined the scrapings left over on the tip of his tee. "Well then Little Man, you better win and you better win quick."

When it was my turn on the tee I hit a huge hook that looked like my ball was going to fly off the planet until it curved left, landed in the fairway and rolled thirty yards past all of them. My second shot never got higher than five feet off the ground and landed thirty yards short of the green but the ball skidded and trundled along the earth and ended up four feet from the pin. My good luck tickled the men to no end. They hooted and hollered and one of them yelled, "That there shot's what I call a Sister-in-Law . . . you're up there next to the hole but you shouldn't be!"

I had a four-foot putt for birdie and drained it to win twenty bucks for the longest drive, twenty for closest to the pin, twenty for the bird and twenty for winning the hole outright since the other three guys all made bogey. Eighty bucks from each player. The men thought the whole thing was a riot and that I was "the luckiest SOB alive." That was the trick, making the good shots look bad.

To round out the act I played with a rickety set of golf clubs and wore sneakers instead of golf shoes. I always used my real putter though because golf is won and lost on the putting green. My putter is a custom-made Scotty Cameron with SILLE engraved on the back, which I always thought was a play on the word *silly*. I've searched every rare golf club website and never saw another putter like it. I found it in the basement when Alicia and I moved back from

Aspen. Mom said she bought it at a garage sale and was going to give it to me for my birthday. I believed her and even felt guilty about ruining her surprise.

Another trick to hustling was not winning too much too fast and always being on the edge of disaster. I knew which sand traps were easy to get out of and I'd hit into them on purpose. I'd pop up drives on short par 4s or slice into the wrong fairway as long as it was still inbounds and had a decent angle to the green.

On top of all the side bets we were playing a skins match so if no one won the hole outright the pot carried over to the next hole. So when Warren's disciples were struggling I'd chunk a chip shot or yank a putt; the key was looking lucky and always letting them think they had a chance. But they didn't and I walked off the eighteenth green with a thousand dollars in my pocket and the name of a greasy spoon in Nebraska that made the best steak and eggs on either side of the Mississippi.

The men were mystified. One of them wondered aloud what their boss would think but they all agreed not to say anything. Before they left, the man who'd been cleaning his fingernails asked to see my putter. He examined it closely and asked, "Where'd you get this?"

"Garage sale," I replied.

"Whadcha pay for it?"

"Three bucks."

"I'll give you five hundred dollars cash money for it right here right now."

"No can do, Kemosabe."

A big ol' hay-chewin' grin eclipsed the midwesterner's face and he said, "Perhaps you didn't hear me. I said five hundred dollars cash money."

"You can say it a third time but it still ain't gonna change my mind."

The three men looked at each other and hucked their way into their rented Escalade and headed back to the hotel a little cash poorer but memory rich. Lu waited for me in his office and I handed him a fifty-dollar bill. On an average day I typically won around three or four hundred dollars. Lu looked at the bill and said, "What's this?"

"Your cut."

"Where's the rest of it?"

"They were good."

"Fifty bucks? Do you know who those guys work for?"

"Some guy named Warren. I think he's a food critic." Lu crumpled up the fifty and threw it at me. I caught it with one hand and said, "What? You don't want it?"

He looked like I had insulted him and asked, "What the hell am I gonna do with fifty bucks?"

"Buy some prunes." I raised my eyebrows and in Lu's phony Confucius voice I said, "Man who eat many prunes get good run for money." Then I hucked like a madman and Lu pointed at the door and yelled for me to get out.

I smoothed out Lu's portrait of Grant as I walked through the pro shop and slid it into my pocket with the rest of my fold. Lu had five hundred bucks coming to him but I didn't feel badly about lying. It was his idea.

But I did feel bad about lying to Mel. We met that night for dinner at Lucky's, a diner that rocked a fifties theme with red and white checkered curtains on the windows, and walls decorated with black-and-white posters of Elvis, James Dean and other famous people from that era whose names we didn't know. Mel always ordered the Grilled American Bandstand Cheese and I always got the Hound Dog Hotdog. She'd get a Diet Coke and me a vanilla shake. It was an easy place to hang out and when we didn't feel like going to the library we'd study there. I was trying to memorize the names of the different treaties between the United States and the American Indians and Mel was feeling neglected. "I think you're the only guy I know who likes to study on a date," she said and reached for my shake.

"This is a date?" I asked without looking up.

"You just bought me dinner."

"I always buy you dinner."

"I know. Those were dates too."

I kept my eyes on my book and said, "I had no idea we were so serious."

Mel took a final tug on my milk shake until there was nothing left and it slurped. "How would you? It's not like we're having sex or anything." This got me to look up and she said, "Oh, there he is. Hello."

"You wanna talk about sex?"

"No. I don't want to talk about sex. All we do is talk about sex. I want to have sex, Gates. With you and only you but at this rate we're gonna be thirty before we even lose our virginity." Melanie desperately wanted to shed her V-Card and it was a major problem because I loved her too much to sleep with her. Mel was convinced I thought she was fat, ugly and flat-chested but none of that was true. I was actually very attracted to Melanie but I couldn't sleep with her until she knew the real me but the only problem was as soon as she knew the real me she wouldn't want to sleep with me anymore. This is what kept me up at night and prevented me from getting boners whenever we kissed. Unlike the truth, a flaccid penis is impossible to hide and every time Mel slid her hand down my pants my sagging state stole a small piece of her self-confidence, which made me feel like the worst kind of criminal.

Fortunately Wade's parents came through the door and stole the spotlight. They ate at Lucky's as much as we did and on nights like that one when they came in late they'd split a shake and stare into each other's eyes. We watched them take their regular table beneath the picture of James

Dean sitting on the hood of a sports car smoking a ciga-rette and then Mel leaned across the table and whispered, "I'm tired of waiting."

"I know. But I want it to be perfect."

"It won't be. That's what practice is for."

I leaned across the table to kiss her but my elbow landed on the tines of a fork and catapulted it into the air. I tried to catch it and knocked the empty stainless steel milk-shake container into our plates. A guy wearing a clown outfit walking on stilts through a quiet church while playing the tuba would have been more subtle. Ike and Sara looked over and smiled.

I grabbed the fork off the floor and put it on the table and said, "After finals. I promise."

"Fine. Right after finals."

When we left Ike and Sara were holding hands beneath the table. They laughed and stared at each other like hon-eymooners and I got so damn jealous of Wade I started to hate him. I walked Mel home and made out with her at the corner of her street for a long time. She never understood how I was a good kisser for someone who was such a prude but there was a lot she didn't know.

I passed Mom's secret boyfriend's house and could see them watching a movie in his living room. The man never lowered his blinds, which I took as a sign of integrity. Mom was curled up next to him on a sofa and the only light in the room was from the TV. If I had been invited inside I would have joined them in a second. But I kept on walking and stared into our house from across the street. Alicia sat in the window of my bedroom reading. I kept on walking and headed toward Harmony's Rest. The common room there smelled like a bottle of bleach that had been pissed in. The carpet was fraying and the walls needed a fresh coat of paint but it had a great couch for sleeping and it was always very quiet there.

animals

*t*he morning shift at Harmony's Rest started at 6 A.M. and that's when they'd kick me out. Not in a bad way or anything; that was just as far as they could bend the rules. I started sleeping there three months ago when Alicia began seducing me on a nightly basis. That's probably when I should've made the connection between Alicia's behavior and Mom's new boyfriend but there was still a lot of information being kept from me. The only way to stay true to Mel was to get away from home and everyone at Harmony's Rest was cool about it; Phyllis even brought in a pillow and a blanket and stored them in a box behind the front desk for me. She didn't ask any questions; she just told me it was there and left it at that.

From Harmony's Rest I always went to North Boulder

Park and sat on a bench and stared west into the foothills looking for herds of deer. We have a ton of deer in Boulder. They walk right down the street in the middle of the day. One time I saw a couple of does waiting for the traffic light to turn red before they crossed the intersection and that might sound like total BS but it's true. Animals can adapt to anything.

I'd go to the park because I didn't want to go home but it was also a great place to people-watch. The same folks were usually there doing the same thing at the same time. One lady would roller-skate around and around the park. She had blond hair that hung down past her butt and she always wore neon pink spandex tights and big square headphones from the Stone Age and she'd hum really loudly. She looked funny but in an unfunny way and I felt sad for her. I wondered if she was married and what her husband thought every morning when she'd leave in her pink tights. I really hoped she did have someone because thinking about her climbing up the front steps of her house in her skates and rolling into a dark room with no one there to ask how it was outside always made my heart sink. I dunno why, I didn't even know her but sometimes things like that get stuck in my head. I actually followed her home two months ago and waited outside her house to see if someone else lived there but I didn't see anyone. Every once in a while I buy a funny card at the pharmacy and send it to her. She has no idea who they're from but hopefully they make her smile anyway.

Another person in the park every morning was this Down's syndrome kid who'd walk this real mangy-looking dog and it probably shouldn't have gotten me down because it was sweet and all to see this handicapped kid with his little four-legged friend but it always bummed me out. For starters the boy never wore a shirt even when it was freezing and he had really pale skin that got all splotchy from the cold. I'd wave and say hi but he was usually mumbling to himself and didn't notice me and then I'd feel guilty I was born normal and he wasn't, especially when I'd think about all the bad things I'd done. I could never decide if I felt bad for the dog or not. There was no question that the kid really loved that mutt but sometimes he'd yell at it or yank his leash really hard for no reason. The dog put up with it pretty well though. Animals can be smart, like those deer, and maybe he knew his owner couldn't really help it and was caring for him as best as he could.

But the park wasn't all depressing. I wouldn't have gone there if it was. Two men would meet there and they always had a cup of coffee in one hand and were pushing baby strollers in the other. They each had a little girl and when it was cold the kids were bundled up in fleece and slippers and round little hats that were on crooked half the time. That always cracked me up seeing those baby girls with

their hats on all sideways sipping juice from a plastic cup
and leaving a trail of Cheerios everywhere they went. They
were too young to talk but they'd make these sounds back
and forth and then bust out giggling and if that doesn't
make you smile you're in for a pretty long life.

That morning after Lucky's I sat on my bench and
scanned the foothills for deer but mostly I was just trying
to figure out how I was gonna explain everything to Mel.
Then the two dads showed up and took their girls from
their strollers and plopped them right down on their feet
and just like that the little girls were toddling around
spraying mini fistfuls of Cheerios all over the place. It
almost made me cry and I don't care how gay that makes
me sound because it was cool. It was a moment. It had
meaning and then I felt like a total schmuck because while
those two little girls were learning how to walk I was still
sitting on that park bench hiding from my life.

So I went right home and poured myself a glass of orange
juice in the kitchen and waited. Alicia walked in a few moments later wearing a cream silk robe over turquoise lingerie. She had already showered and was wearing makeup and
her hair was perfect. The robe was tied at her waist and
barely went below her hips. She stopped a few feet away
from me and said, "You didn't come home last night."

"I studied late at Timmy Timmy Timmy's so I crashed
there."

"I was worried about you." She looked out the window. "How is it outside?"

"It's nice."

Alicia reached across me to grab the carton of orange juice. She smelled like the perfume she always wore. Her robe was tied loosely and falling open at her boobs. She caught me staring at them and said, "How's the studying coming?"

"I dunno." I looked away. "I got a lot on my mind, you know?"

"Like what?"

"Like everything I've been trying to talk to you about for the past three months."

Alicia cupped my face with her hands and said, "You worry too much."

"I feel guilty."

"There's nothing to feel guilty about." She grabbed my glass, filled it with OJ and offered me a sip. I declined. "Haven't we been through this a million times?" she asked.

"It's different now. I'm with Melanie. When we lived in Aspen I didn't have a girlfriend."

"When we lived in Aspen you were a walking erection." Alicia took a final sip of juice and placed the glass gently on the counter. She leaned forward, pecked me on the lips and said, "Good luck with your tests," then went back up-stairs to get dressed.

Exams went just dandy. It's been ten days and school

hasn't called to tell me I have to drop out or take summer classes so I must have passed. Timmy Timmy Timmy and I hung around after the last test and played paper football across our teacher's desk. The halls were quiet because everyone was gone and it was so peaceful the school felt like it was a thousand times bigger and that 3T's and I were just two specks in a huge maze. If you ever get a chance to hang out in a deserted school building do it. It's a lot like sitting in an empty church. Sometimes you just don't realize how quiet the world can be until you hear it for yourself.

"So I guess it's officially summer," I said as I slid the small paper triangle toward 3T's' side of the desk. That's how you play paper football, by folding up a piece of paper into a small tight triangle and sliding it across a tabletop, trying to make it stop while hanging over the edge. Sounds boring but if you play with someone you like it just becomes part of the conversation. Timmy Timmy Timmy nodded at my comment and I said, "So when do you take off?" 3T's was leaving for three weeks of jobs in New York, North Carolina and Houston. He was bummed about going to Houston but the shoot was a television ad for an allergy medicine that was going to air on like every channel from November through May, which 3T's said is the equivalent of winning a small lottery.

Timmy Timmy Timmy replied, "Tomorrow tomorrow tomorrow," and shot the football across the desk. Then he said, "I hope you figure it out while I'm gone gone gone."

"What's that?"

He gave me this weird long look. He could talk with his eyes and they were saying he knew something was wrong and was worried. I actually debated spilling my guts to him right then and there. Who better to confess your sins to than a guy with a speech impediment who's practically mute and about to leave town?

3T's took a deep breath and said, "Gates, if you don't think I don't know you've been walking around with a secret secret secret then you must not think I'm very smart smart smart. I'm your friend and you can tell me anything and I'll always have your back because I know you got mine mine mine." He let out a huge sigh.

I wanted to hug him but that would have been gay so I reached my arm across the desk and we punched fists, which was basically our version of hugging anyway. Fortunately Melanie showed up, because my eyes were getting tingly and as soon as she appeared in the doorway I calmed down and that's when I knew I loved her for sure and it practically dropped me. Melanie was wearing a pair of khaki shorts and a Bob Marley T-shirt that said *Everything's gonna be alright* beneath the singer's picture and just seeing her made me believe those words.

3T's gave me another long look. He had said his piece and we both knew it so he nodded goodbye to Mel and she blew him a kiss and winked. Mel could be kinda corny like that but she could pull it off. Sometimes I think that's what love really is: not giving a deuce if your chick acts like a dweeb.

We watched Timmy Timmy Timmy leave and then Mel ran up to me with little tiny steps and threw her arms around my waist and said, "Summer's here!"

"How'd your final go?" I asked after giving her a hug and a kiss.

"Terrible. I could barely concentrate. All I could think about was what I'd be doing *after* the test." She bit her lower lip and grinned.

I wanted so badly for her innuendo to give me a boner but nothing happened. Nothing ever happened with Mel. I just felt too guilty.

"Ready?" she asked.

I nodded and we walked out through the school doors and into our summer vacation together. Mel wanted to go swimming but I told her I had to go into town and do an errand for Mom and she reminded me to come over to her house that night and we both knew what that meant.

Boulder High School is just a couple of blocks from downtown and I only had a few minutes to psych myself up so to buy a little time I locked my bike outside Alicia's office and sat on a bench on Pearl Street. It was the middle of June and hot as balls, and sweat was running down both sides of my body. My palms were as wet as my mouth was dry and I couldn't stop tapping my foot. I sat across from

Go Fly A Kite, which was a store that believe it or not sold kites. People always talked about the place because it was one of the last independently owned shops on the Pearl Street Mall, which I guess was some kind of big deal. The paper was always griping about how much town was changing and that there were no places left for the mom-and-pop stores but if no one was shopping there in the first place what did it matter anyway?

I was staring at the window of this kite shop and out walked Ike and Sara Peterson. They didn't buy a kite and they smiled when they noticed me and walked right over. For retired famous people Ike and Sara did a heck of a job blending in with the rest of the town. He had on a golf shirt and pleated shorts and she was wearing a big straw hat to stay out of the sun. People barely ever recognized them and that's one of the reasons they're always so happy. Life can be a real ballbreaker like that. First they both worked really hard to get famous and then they had to do everything short of hiring a shape-shifter just to have a regular life. Ike and Sara were all smiles and Sara said, "Congratulations! You're now officially a senior in high school!"

I stood up to greet them. "Thanks, I feel ten times cooler already."

"We saw you with Melanie last night." Sara smiled all coy. "Hold on to that one." Ike nodded in agreement.

I couldn't help myself and had to brag. "You know she

can drive the ball two hundred and fifty yards, straight as an arrow."

Ike said, "Damn," like he was impressed and then he said, "Hey, you and me should play sometime but you gotta give me a bunch of strokes because I'm a twelve handicap."

I couldn't believe Ike Peterson was asking me to play golf. I wondered if either he or Sara knew I gave Wade the panties that sent him to the ER. "Sure thing," I said. "How much you wanna play for?"

He laughed. "You want to play for money? Okay, how about twenty bucks?"

"A hole?"

That made him laugh even harder. "Right . . . twenty bucks a hole." He kicked my sneaker softly before he and Sara headed down the street. He hasn't gotten in touch with me yet but it's only been ten days. Even if he just wanted to play for a dollar I doubt I'd take the bet. I'm trying not to do that stuff anymore after everything that happened. Ike won't call for a while anyway because right now he's probably in a distant land hiding Wade from the mess we made.

It was weird thinking how Ike had a golf handicap and that Sara was worried about getting too much sun. It gave me hope I could change too and I got up and went to Alicia's office with a new confidence. A mother and her son were in the waiting room and they were kinda surprised to see someone else at their shrink's office. I was feeling good, almost a little too good, and I turned to the little guy and said, "What are ya in for?" like we were cellmates or something.

He had these huge brown eyes and freckles on the bridge of his nose and he looked at me real cool and said, "I pissed all over my stepmother's closet."

"Ouch. That's like ten to fifteen sessions even with good behavior."

He glanced at his mom and said, "I won't do more than ten." Then he flipped up his comic book and went back to reading.

I laughed and looked at his mother and she was actually laughing too and said, "You see what I'm dealing with here?"

Alicia opened the door and froze when she saw me. I had managed to catch her off guard and it felt good, like I was in control. She wore a black skirt and a black long-sleeve button-down shirt. The skirt had two huge white buttons on the waistline and stretched well below her knees.

"Gates . . ." Fake smile. "What are you doing here?" I stood up and walked into her office. Alicia said to the mother, "I'm sorry, this'll only take a second."

I lay down on the couch and stared up at the ceiling and she shut the door and hissed, "This is totally inappropriate. Those people deserve privacy and you know that. I'm not running a dentist's office here."

Alicia rarely lost her cool and I was feeling kinda cocky knowing I had taken her off her game. "What's with the buttons?" I asked her.

"You mean my skirt? It's cute."

"You look like a domino."

Alicia was still standing by the door and I was dying to sit up and see her reaction but I kept staring at the ceiling. The room got very quiet and then she said, "What do you want Gates?"

"I'm sleeping with Melanie tonight but first I'm going to tell her about us and you can't talk me out of it so don't bother."

"I wouldn't do that. She'll never talk to you again."

"She likes me. And I like her."

"And I like hamburgers but none of that matters. Do you honestly think she'll understand? And what if she starts telling her friends? It's a small town and sooner or later even your mom would get wind."

"I don't care if Mom finds out. It would actually be a relief."

"She'll kill herself. Want that on your shoulders?"

"Mom's a lot better now. She's got a boyfriend, she just sold a big house, she'll be alright."

"She's never going to be alright. How many times do I have to tell you that, Gates? Your mother is a sick, sick woman."

I had been in Alicia's office one time before when I was twelve and got in trouble at school. "Hey you were my shrink once, let me ask you a question. Why can't I get a boner with Melanie but all you have to do is touch me?" It was a fucked-up thing to ask but I wanted the answer and Alicia was the only person who could give it to me, which is why I went to her office in the first place.

Alicia jiggled my foot and said, "Pavlov's response."

I lifted up my head to see her. "You mean like the dog?"

"I'm kidding," she smiled and we both kinda laughed.

The woman could disarm me in an instant and lying on the couch joking around was a reminder she was the closest thing to a parent I ever had. Sometimes I think I slept with her just to make sure she'd keep caring for me because Mom didn't know how and I had no father. Sometimes I did it to rebel against living in a house where morals and china were broken thoughtlessly. And sometimes I fucked Alicia because I knew the guilt would torment me and I felt like I deserved a life of suffering for kissing her in the first place.

Alicia asked, "Do you have a hard-on right now?"

"No." But I got one as soon as she asked.

She sat next to me and I wanted to push her off the couch or scream for the mother in the waiting room but I was frozen. I opened my mouth to say something but Alicia shushed me and said everything was going to be alright as she unzipped my pants and straddled my waist.

She was always so wet and I was always so hard and getting inside her was about as easy as sliding a hot knife through a warm stick of butter.

Afterward she made a show of retrieving her underwear. They were all the way over by the door so she must have taken them off right after I had walked in the room. At the time I had felt so cocky and in control. She grinned as she threaded her ankles through the leg holes of her panties and pulled them up beneath her skirt. She wasn't smiling at me, she was smiling to herself, not from the sex I had given her but from the sex she had gotten.

When I left the waiting room I stopped at the door and watched the little pisser enter Alicia's office. His mom was looking at me funny because my eyes were all red. I did my best to smile and said, "Don't worry, people really can change."

One of the beautiful things about golf is that it can be just as much a practice of meditation as it can be a sport. When I left Alicia's office I needed to blank out so I rode over to the BGC and found my own private little Idaho on the far side of the range. I must have hit about two hundred balls and during that time I didn't once think about Alicia, Mom, Melanie or even myself. It was a good escape but when I quit nothing had changed. Alicia was still giving me boners and I was still giving in to her and I could only blame myself. I only had a few hours until the cherry-popping ceremony at Melanie's and I didn't know what I was going to do.

I went to the caddy shack and bought a soda from the machine and the can exploded and sprayed all over the front of my shirt. The club has a lost-and-found that's mostly filled with head covers and bag towels but I managed to dig up a yellow sweater with a piano keyboard going straight up the middle of the chest with black musical notes peppered along the sleeves and the back. It had been sitting in there for months. Someone's wife probably gave it to them for Christmas and they conveniently "forgot" it at the course.

I thought I'd change in Lu's office and rather than walk through the pro shop looking like a soda machine barfed on me, I went the back way through the stockroom. Right when I got to Lu's office a man knocked on the door from the pro shop side. He was wearing a suit and carrying a briefcase and looked very serious so I stepped back out of sight rather than interrupt.

"Hey Lu," the man said. He really didn't seem all that happy to be there.

"Paul." Lu stood up to shake his hand. "You come to play?"

"Unfortunately, no."

"How's Molly?"

"She's good. She's good. What about Cynthia? She driving you crazy with the wedding plans?"

I was about to leave and change in the bathroom even though caddies aren't allowed in the locker room but Lu had never talked about getting married or a girlfriend named Cynthia so I stuck around.

Lu motioned for Paul to sit and said, "Actually, Cynthia moved out."

Paul took his seat. "Oh, I'm sorry."

"Can I get you something to drink? Bottle of water? Beer?"

"No thanks. We need to talk."

Lu sat down. "I know I'm late Paul."

"You're more than late. You've missed three payments and you're about to miss a fourth."

Lu unlocked one of the lower drawers on his desk and pulled out a brick of money. "Here's five thousand."

Paul didn't reach for it. "That's not even a quarter of what you owe and do you really expect me to carry that thing around? You gotta come down to the bank, Lu. Deposit what you can and maybe we can give you another month or two but you can't put it off any longer." Paul slid a piece of paper across Lu's desk but it wasn't folded into a little triangle and they weren't playing any games. He got up and left and they didn't punch fists or even say goodbye.

Once Paul was gone Lu said, "You can come in now Gates."

I peered around the doorway. "Sorry, I didn't want to interrupt."

Lu waved it off and in his Chinaman voice said, "Man who fart in church sit in own pew."

"Who's Cynthia?"

"That guy's a Melvin. How 101 can you get being a mortgage broker?"

I didn't understand the question or whether it was even a question at all so I just stood there holding that ugly sweater in my hand.

Lu didn't like the silence and he massaged his chin with mock thought and in his Confucius voice declared, "Wise man never play leapfrog with unicorn."

I didn't laugh. I never liked Lu's jokes. He was still uncomfortable and pointed at the sweater and said, "Wha'cha got there?" He was trying way too hard to pretend like everything was great and it only made the situation more awkward.

I held up the sweater like a flag and said, "I got it out of the lost-and-found. I'll bring it back tomorrow."

Lu shielded his eyes and said, "Don't ever bring that thing back here again." He pointed into the pro shop. "Grab a new shirt off the rack. It's on the house." He sprung out of his chair and like Confucius said, "Foolish man give wife grand piano, wise man give wife upright organ," then trotted out of the office to keep things from getting worse. He'd made three Confucius jokes in a row, which meant he was extremely uncomfortable.

I suddenly felt very guilty for not giving him his cut from the day before. I never considered he might have a mortgage or phony wedding to pay for. My shirt was already getting sticky from the soda and I peeled it off and threw on the sweater. It was itchy and smelled like Old Spice. The temperature outside was way too hot for wool but I wasn't gonna take one of Lu's shirts. He couldn't really afford to give me one anyway.

I definitely wanted to change but I didn't want to go home and see Alicia so the only option was to show up at Mel's dressed like a gay piano. When Mel answered the door she was fresh out of the shower and her hair was wet and neatly brushed. She had switched out of her shorts and Bob Marley tee and into a simple white cotton sundress with daisies along the bottom trim. She busted out laughing when she saw the sweater and asked, "Are you stealing Bill Cosby's clothes again?"

"I thought we were hanging out tonight."

She took a moment to choose her words. "We are but you gotta go home and change." She tugged the sweater. "I'm gonna remember this night for the rest of my life and I don't want this image following me around forever."

She was so vulnerable, all caught up in what I was gonna wear for the big night that I blurted out, "Mel there's something I have to tell you first."

Melanie grabbed my hands and stepped close so our toes touched. "Gates, there are a few things that girls spend a lot of time fantasizing about. One is our wedding day. One is our dream house. And one is the night we lose our virginity." She lowered her head and pecked my lips. "So before you say anything just think about that."

"You really want everything to be just right don't you?"

She shrugged. "I know I'm being dumb, but please?"

"You're not being dumb at all. I'll go change right now." I gave her a kiss and headed home wishing it could be that easy.

When I got to my house I called Mel and told her Mom wasn't feeling well and needed me to stay home. It was a lie I knew she wouldn't challenge. Alicia walked into the kitchen when I hung up and casually said, "I'm gonna make something yummy for dinner, you hungry?" She was still wearing her domino outfit and I wanted to knock her over.

I looked her in the eyes and said, "This is ruining my life."

She took a deep breath. "Do you want to stop doing it?"

"Of course I want to stop. You already know that."

She shrugged and replied, "Then stop."

"It'd be a whole lot easier if you didn't throw yourself at me," I said.

She laughed and replied, "Fine. Blame it on me."

"Well it's true."

"Don't worry, Gates. I'm moving out in a few days anyway so pretty soon it'll just be you and." Alicia slowly looked all around the kitchen. Then she said, "I guess it'll just be you."

I went up to my room and after a while I smelled food cooking in the kitchen and it smelled like the pasta Alicia made for Halloween the year we lived in Aspen. We'd only been there two months but I was already obsessed with her. Nothing sexual had passed between us yet but I had masturbated myself to sleep many a night as I spied on her while she relaxed nude in the hot tub beneath my bedroom window. That Halloween we didn't get trick-or-treaters because Alicia turned off the lights and lowered the blinds. She had bought us costumes. I was dressed as a doctor and she as a nurse, but the kind in music videos and not hospitals.

The food was really cooking downstairs and my mouth started to water. Then I got so horny I fished out a pair of Alicia's panties I hid beneath my T-shirts. I thought about Melanie and all the reasons I loved her but it was the scent of the food simmering below that made me cum.

some lies were meant to be told

$t$he next morning I showered and crept down to the kitchen for a quick breakfast and Alicia showed up minutes later in a gray business suit. She gave my shoulders a friendly squeeze and went out the door. The whole transaction was so normal it didn't seem real and I rode to the BGC wondering if our time together in Aspen had even happened.

The Vanleers' car was in the parking lot, which meant I'd be looping for them. I was their designated caddy and for a while it was a great arrangement. Melanie's parents were good to me and were the most popular members at the club so having their bag put me at the top of the caddy food chain. That changed a few months ago when Mr. Vanleer started drinking on the course. The more he drank the more handsy he got, not with his swing but with my butt cheeks. Mrs. Vanleer never seemed to notice but the caddies took heed and I went from holding court in the caddy shack to being nicknamed Fun Buns. At first I didn't mind the teasing but Mr. Vanleer didn't stop and the ribbing didn't stop so it's no wonder I snapped and did what I did.

I went to the storage room to get my caddy bib and heard Lu swearing in his office so I poked my head in and saw European football on the TV. Lu was wearing a bright pink shirt with a starched collar and a pair of madras shorts and I said to him, "Dude, why don't you just go for it and change your name to Brewster." He shushed me and a team scored off a penalty kick and he cursed and threw a pen at the TV.

"Please tell me you didn't bet on this," I said.

"A few grand, I had a good line."

"A good line? You don't know shit about soccer."

"It was a good line."

"You gonna beat it?"

Lu stretched his shirt to cover his belly. The corners of his mouth rose and like Confucius he said, "Man who scratch ass should not bite fingernail." He walked to the TV and pulled its cord from the wall and the screen popped before it went dark. Then he said, "The Vanleers are already on the range, Fun Buns. You should probably get out there."

Marty Vanleer is sixty-five years young and Mrs. Vanleer is forty-one years old. Marty was born and bred in Du-
rango, Colorado, and is as big and sturdy as a pine tree.
Mrs. Vanleer was born in Baton Rouge, Louisiana, and is as
prim and proper as a doily. She came to Boulder to get her
law degree and by that point Marty was a big-time lawyer
who volunteered at the University one semester a year to
teach an ethics course. Mrs. Vanleer was in his class so he
was either a shitty teacher or she was a poor student because when they crossed drunken paths one night Right
and Wrong were tossed out the window and the conse-
quence was Melanie's conception. The Vanleers were
forced into marriage and never truly in love but showered
their daughter with adoration and affection and until re-
cently didn't once fight in front of her so maybe they did
know a thing or two about ethics after all.

When I got to the range they stopped practicing and
welcomed me like one of their own. "There he is," Marty
said. "We missed you last night. Mel said you were coming
over one minute and then the next minute you weren't."

"Is your mother feeling better?" Mrs. Vanleer asked.
There was something different about her but I couldn't
figure out what. It had been over a month since she'd
played golf and this was the first time I had seen her in several weeks.

"She's fine, thank you." I was always well-mannered

around Mel's mother. Her civility was contagious. I knew they knew about Mom's history with mental illness. The Vanleers knew all. Mrs. Vanleer was on the board of every charity in town and Marty was on the board of every business in town. If our city was a prom they'd have been the king and queen.

Mrs. Vanleer stood with a very straight back, her chin was lifted, and there was definitely something different about her posture but I couldn't figure out what. "And how is your mother's friend Alicia?" She asked in a way that made the question sound loaded. "Is she still living with you all?"

"She is." I couldn't look her in the eye.

"They have such a great relationship, it's wonderful."

I rifled through Mrs. Vanleer's golf clubs to see if any needed to be cleaned, but that just made our silence more awkward.

Mrs. Vanleer stood as still as a statue, almost as if she was posing. "You know I've invited Alicia to join the boards of several charities I'm involved with but she always declines. She's very reclusive, that one."

"I think she likes it that way," I said.

"It's too bad. She obviously has a lot to offer."

I hated it when people spoke highly of Alicia. It happened all the time and it discouraged me even more from trying to tell anyone about what happened in Aspen because I knew she'd deny it and her word would be more trusted than mine.

"What do you say we go play?" Marty asked and bounded toward the first tee before anyone could answer. I grabbed their bags and trailed a few feet behind. Wade was watching from the practice green. He pointed at Marty and mimicked the act of fellatio by pumping his fist toward his mouth and popping out his cheek with his tongue. I replied by scratching my nose with my middle finger. Then I realized what was different about Mrs. Vanleer—her clothes. She was wearing a short skirt and a tight sleeveless top. Normally she wore long baggy pants, a long-sleeved shirt, a glove on each hand and a wide-brimmed hat. This one caddy named Tap Water because he wore ugly shirts and had no taste said Mrs. Vanleer was an ice woman and would melt if the sun hit her skin. None of the caddies thought she was sexy and they all worshipped Marty and couldn't fathom why he married such a gnat pigeon. Another caddy, Frostbite (lost two toes on a camping trip), described her as a cross between an aspen tree and a trout. I agreed but Timmy Timmy Timmy thought otherwise. He had a huge crush on Mrs. Vanleer and asked about her constantly and would make up excuses for us to stop by Mel's house. Mrs. Vanleer lit up when 3T's was around and always made a point of saying hello. One time Mel busted her changing into a sexier outfit when 3T's was there.

To Timmy Timmy Timmy's credit, seeing Mrs. Vanleer in her new wardrobe changed my mind. Not only were her legs pretty nice but her ass was downright perky and it appeared as if she had gotten a boob job. That day was the great unveiling, which explained why she was so chatty on the range. There'd been a decent group of people practicing and she wanted them all to notice.

We breezed through the front nine and when we made the turn Marty decided to get a cart and four Bloody Marys. He needed the cart to hold the drinks so I drove and by the thirteenth hole they both had a nice buzz. Two holes later Marty had more drinks delivered out and I had to make sure not to stand within arm's reach of him.

When we were done I pulled Marty aside and said, "Sir, forgive me if I'm being rude but maybe you shouldn't drink so much on the course. You shot a forty-two on the front and a sixty on the back."

Marty pressed his hands together, looked at me inquisitively and asked, "Have you ever given a foot massage? I've given a million foot massages and they all meant something." He pulled out a fat wad of cash.

I was in no mood so I didn't mince words. "Mr. Vanleer, I don't think I should caddy for you anymore. When you get drunk you get very touchy-feely and it makes me uncomfortable; especially since I'm in love with your daughter."

He counted out ten twenty-dollar bills and handed them to me. Then he said, "That's pride fucking with you. Fuck pride." He pressed the money into my hand. "Pride only hurts, it never helps." Then he said, "So we're Kool and the Gang, right?" and strolled away.

Procto (his index finger is brown from a birthmark) and Mexican (is Caucasian but has dark skin) were waiting for a loop in the caddy shack. Procto's favorite joke was to ask if I cleaned Marty's balls with a wet towel or my tongue and Mexican's choice line was to remind me to wear tighter shorts and no underwear next time Marty plays. I was dying to talk to neither of them so I ran to my bike and split with no real destination in mind.

I ended up on the bench across from Go Fly A Kite. There was a GOING OUT OF BUSINESS sign in the window that hadn't been there the day before. A street performer whose act was to fold his body into a tiny clear box was doing lunges and back bends to prepare for his show. He had dreads and talked with an island accent and was always smiling. How he ever figured out that squeezing into a small box was his life's calling I'll never know but people loved his show. He was chatting with everyone passing by and all I could think about was how nice it must feel to make so many people happy every day.

I was looking around for Alicia because I kinda wanted to talk to her and make sure she wasn't going to move out or anything. Alicia always threatened to leave when she was fighting with Mom and she was the only person who kept Mom grounded, so as much as Alicia was ruining my life I needed her. When I was twelve Mom and Alicia got in a fight after I got suspended from school for carving WHORE into my teacher's desk. My teacher was a woman and everyone assumed I was talking about her but after seeing me as a patient Alicia (correctly) determined my etching was aimed at Mom and that I needed more attention at home. Mom took the analysis well. She smashed a hammer through Alicia's windshield and locked herself in her room and didn't come out for six days and refused to talk through the door. I missed a week of school and ate cereal for every meal until we ran out of milk. There was no bread in the house so I made peanut butter and jelly sandwiches on taco shells and melted American cheese on waffles. Then Mom slit her wrists in the middle of the night and called Alicia for help. After that it was clear to all three of us that Mom needed Alicia in her life to stay alive.

Mom would sometimes test herself and force distance between her and Alicia. She knew how much she relied on her and resented being so dependent. Even after Alicia officially moved in with us Mom would disappear for long weekends or ten-day vacations. I never understood why Alicia put up with it. Sometimes I thought she felt a responsibility to look after me but after our year in Aspen, whenever Mom left us alone we'd fuck the entire time she was gone. So Alicia couldn't have been too worried about my welfare because I always resisted the sex, but it was hard to be convincing with a raging boner. They always fought right before Mom's trips, which were often unannounced until the day of her departure. Hearing them argue would fill me with dread and lust both at the same time. Just seeing Mom's suitcase by the door would make me hard.

I hung out on the bench for an hour and watched the Rasta do his show. He had set out a yellow, green and red striped knit hat for tips so I gave him a twenty and went into Go Fly A Kite and bought a wind chime. On my way to Harmony's Rest I snuck by the roller-skating lady's house and hung it on her porch.

Cliff was waiting on the front steps of the home. He recognized the sound of my bike and immediately pleaded for me to read a new book. I told him Phyllis would have my ass and he kept saying, "For the greater good, Gates. For the greater good. We're not dead yet." I locked my arm in his and we walked to the dining room. Cliff was sullen but when we pushed through the swinging doors into the eating hall he knew a small group would be waiting and even though he couldn't see the gathering he instantly perked up and said to the crowd, "Hey, how do you make a sweet old lady swear . . . Tell the sweet old lady sitting next to her to shout bingo!"

61

No one laughed. He told that joke almost every week. Five minutes into *The Awakening* everyone was snoozing, even Cliff. It was sad to see them so sedated so I decided to bring in a new book the next day because some lies were meant to be told.

When I got home Mom's car was in the driveway and Alicia's wasn't, which was very unusual. The house was empty and all the lights were off and when I called out for Mom she didn't answer. Her bedroom door was closed but her hair dryer buzzed from her bathroom so I knocked loudly and entered her bedroom slowly to not startle her. She was wearing white jeans, a yellow tank top and sandals and her eyes were closed as she brushed the warm air through her damp hair. When she saw me she jumped and was annoyed I had snuck up on her.

"Sorry!" I yelled over the noise. "I knocked but you couldn't hear me."

Mom turned off the dryer and held it at her hip. "What's up?"

"Nothing. I just wanted to say hi."

"No golf tonight?"

"I wasn't in the mood. You heading out?"

Mom smiled unenthusiastically and said, "A bunch of people from the office are going to watch our boss sing jazz at some club in Lafayette."

"Right on. Is she any good?"

Mom rolled her eyes. "Gotta go though."

We laughed and everything seemed cool so I said, "Are you dragging your boyfriend with you or does he get a pass?"

Mom looked back at the mirror, flipped on the blow dryer and brushed her hair. I unplugged the cord and it made a loud pop that startled Mom so badly she dropped the dryer and it smashed into pieces on the marble floor. Mom shouted, "Are you trying to kill me!"

I softened my voice because when Mom Bitchzilla'd that would calm her down. "All we ever do is lie and I'm sick of it," I said.

"Great, so now I'm a liar."

"I just don't understand why you pretend like you don't have a boyfriend."

"Who?"

"The guy down the street."

"There's nothing to know."

"I think it's great you like someone and if you're happy I'm happy."

"I'm doing the best I can. Sorry if that's not good enough."

"Who says it isn't good enough?"

"I can see it every time you look at me," she said.

"Sometimes I just wish we could tell each other things, you know?"

Mom sighed. Her eyes pleaded with me to change the subject. "I don't have an answer for that," she finally replied.

We looked at each other with nothing to say except everything. "Anyway . . . ," I said.

"Did you get in a fight with Alicia? She's threatening to move out again." Mom waved her hand like she didn't really believe her and added, "I'm sure it's nothing."

"She's been acting kinda weird lately," I said.

"How so?"

"Oh you know, she just gets a little antsy when you're not around and ever since you've been hanging out down the street she's been a lot more . . . present."

"Present?"

"Because it's just me and her every night."

"If you don't like it then tell her."

"Don't like what?"

Mom shrugged. "I don't know, her presence."

Her presence was a euphemism to end all euphemisms. Mom spoke the words in a way that suggested she knew but I convinced myself this wasn't possible because I didn't want to believe Mom would ignore her best friend molesting me.

"Mrs. Vanleer made a funny comment to me today," I ventured.

"Oh Jesus, not *that* woman," Mom said.

"She was asking about you and Alicia and she kinda made it seem like you guys were a couple."

"Let me tell you something about women like Mrs. Vanleer: when their little minds aren't distracted by yoga, or golf or shopping their thoughts run rampant from boredom."

"She was actually trying to be nice," I said.

"By insinuating to my son I'm a lesbian? Next time tell her not to do me any favors."

"She got fake boobs," I offered.

Mom chuckled. "Perfect. Now she's that much closer to becoming a walking cliché. Next thing you know she'll be hitting on you."

I'd never heard Mom go off on Mrs. Vanleer so brutally. She usually talked about how much she liked her. "Actually, it's Mr. Vanleer who keeps grabbing my ass."

Mom laughed so hard she had to steady herself on the bathroom counter.

"It isn't funny," I said, which only made her laugh harder. I'd been hoping for sympathy, or maybe even a shred of advice, but at least Mom was laughing. Victories come in many forms, even when they're losses.

We picked up the pieces of the blow dryer together and when everything was clean Mom handed me the broken handle and said, "You're buying me a new one of these." Then she added, "His name is Stuart and he's not my boyfriend."

I held up both hands and said, "Okay okay. He's not your boyfriend."

Mom gave herself a final look in the mirror and said, "You're on your own tonight because Alicia's got a date so don't stay up late." It was a funny thing for Mom to say because she was basically admitting she wouldn't be coming home, right after denying Stuart was her boyfriend. It kinda made me wonder why I even bothered trying.

Melanie had been kind enough to give me a rain check to say hi to her hymen but I had a few hours to kill so I rode out to Target to get a blow dryer. They had eighteen models and I bought a metallic blue one because blue was Mom's favorite color. The store was crowded and I looked around for Ike and Sara as I walked up and down the aisles because it would have been fun to see them. My basket eventually was filled with a picnic blanket, candles, wineglasses, a bottle of apple cider champagne, a flashlight and a pack of rubbers that I hid under the blanket so no one would see me walking around with them. I had never bought condoms before and it kinda turned me on. I wanted to buy a kite but they were sold out. At home I left Mom's dryer on her pillow, where she wouldn't find it until morning.

I called 3T's on my way to Mel's house with the premise of checking how his flight went but I actually hoped to get the nerve up to explain my dilemma about Mel and Alicia. I'd never been brave enough to confess to him before but thought maybe his being two thousand miles away might make it easier. He answered the phone, "Gator Gator, procrastinator." He always answered by saying my name twice followed by a word that rhymed because he hated saying, "Hello hello hello."

"Procrastinator? Why do you say that?"

"Got a text from Mel Mel Mel. All it said was, 'Your friend's a prude prude prude.'"

Mel texting 3T's meant she was even more hurt than I'd realized. I didn't blame her for being so confused; most guys my age don't back out of having sex. "I flaked on her pretty hard last night," I said. Then there was a long period of silence. I wanted to ask if 3T's was still on the line but didn't want to make him say hello hello hello because he hated it so much so I went with "By the way, Mrs. Vanleer got a boob job; she actually looks kinda hot," because I knew that would get him talking.

"I've been telling you that for years years years. Is that why you called, to tell me about your girlfriend's mother's boobs boobs boobs?"

"Can't I say hi?"

"You can say anything you want want want. That's my point point point."

The best thing about best friends is they know you better than you do yourself. Timmy Timmy Timmy was the best best friend because he had patience and could wait for me to clear my conscious to him. He knew it was just a matter of time. "I'm almost at Mel's," I told him. "I should probably go."

"Say hi to Mrs. Vanleer for me me me."

"That'll make her smile."

He laughed and said, "Just make Melanie smile smile smile," and abruptly hung up because Timmy Timmy Timmy loved having the last word . . . the last three words, actually.

Marty answered the Vanleers' door. He was as bombed as Baghdad and threw his arm in the air and shouted, "Garçon!" and then fell backward onto his ass and couldn't get up. Mrs. Vanleer came running. She was horrified but her hair was perfect and she helped him stand and led him away saying, "Come on, bedtime."

Marty mumbled something about eating blueberry pie for breakfast and when Mel came outside she was so embarrassed she could barely look me in the eye. I grabbed her hand and we walked without saying a word for three blocks. There are times for dumb jokes and then there are times for silence. Mel needed silence. Eventually she said, "Sorry. Dad's been really in to *Pulp Fiction* lately. That's all he does, get drunk and watch *Pulp Fiction* all night. Half the time Mom can't deal with it so she gets drunk too." I laughed because Mel's parents had always been so perfect. Mel said, "I know, right? And get this; Mom woke me up at two in the morning last night rummaging through my desk for batteries. Apparently the ones in her vibrator died and she needed some right away."

"Your mom uses a vibrator?" I stopped walking. We had reached the entrance to Wonderland Lake Park, where I had planned a surprise for her.

"Yup. And she got a boob job too." She skipped a few feet ahead of me and lifted her arms out to the side as if to say, "Top that."

"Yeah . . . I noticed. So did everybody on the range." I gave her a reassuring smile and said, "Follow me." I led us by flashlight to the deepest corner of the park, where I had set up the picnic blanket and the pseudo champagne. Mel was impressed. I lit the candles and placed one on each corner of the blanket. "I don't know how you fantasized about it all your life but I hope this works," I said, holding the wineglasses upside down by their stems the way all the suave guys do on TV.

Mel was smirking, probably because I was clutching the wineglasses like a tool. She sat cross-legged and gazed at the flickering candles, and her parents' unusual behavior was the furthest thing from her mind. I had made her happy. "Won't people see us?" she asked.

"Not once we put out the lights."

She crawled the perimeter of the blanket and blew out each flame then found me in the dark and we began to kiss. We started out slow but things got hot in a hurry and yet there was no wood in my johnson. Mel took her hand out of my pants and said, "What is it?"

"I think I'm freaked out someone'll see us."

"You just said no one'll see us. Besides, it's pitch-black out, there's not even a moon."

We started going at it again and from nowhere I smelled Alicia's pasta. I sat up and said, "Do you smell that?"

Mel sighed loudly and collapsed onto her back. "Smell what?"

"Parmesan cheese and sausage."

"All I smell is a rat. Stop stalling."

"I'm not stalling."

"Well you're not doing anything else either." She sat up and said, "You obviously don't think I'm pretty and you don't want to say it but this is hurting my feelings and I want to go home now."

"Of course I think you're pretty." I tried to hug her but she didn't let me.

"I'm like a foot taller than you and I probably weigh more than you too."

"Just hug me for a second, okay?"

She fell into my arms and then it got nice and quiet and we could feel each other breathing. She calmed down and it was good and I tried to think of something to say but everything I thought of was lame so I played it safe and let my hug do all the work.

Then she said, "Sometimes it's like you're not even here."

"I'm here, Mel. Trust me."

"Well something's missing."

I let her go and said, "There's a lot on my mind right now. Stuff at home," but I had played the Mom card the night before so it didn't ring true.

Mel found the lighter and lit one candle. Softly, kindly, the way I imagined someone who truly loved me would speak to me, she said, "You know you can tell me anything."

"Not this." I started to shake uncontrollably so Mel grabbed my hands. She inched closer and squinted as she struggled to understand what had suddenly turned me into a basket case. Then she lunged at me with a big kiss. She was only trying to make me feel better and her gesture would have been reassuring to any other boy, but I was too shook up and shoved her away harder than necessary, harder than I meant to and hard enough to make her flee. A better soul would have chased her down, begged her to listen and told her the whole nasty truth but I just sat there shaking.

I rolled the candles, wineglasses and bottle of cider up in the blanket and dumped the entire bundle in the trash and rode my bike to the movie theater and waited. An hour later Alicia came out and picked at something in her teeth as she walked toward her car. Next stop was Stuart's garage and Mom's car was hidden there. I thought about getting the hair dryer and putting it on her windshield but leaving it on her pillow was obvious enough. When I got home I walked straight to Alicia's room and opened her door without knocking. She was in bed with a book in her lap and wore reading glasses that made her look old. She turned her gaze from her book to me and very calmly said, "Yeeeeees?"

"Are you moving out?" I asked from the hallway.

"Maybe, maybe not. Stay tuned . . ."

"Fuck you," I said and slammed the door.

Then I stole some pills from Mom's medicine cabinet. I didn't even know what they did and I didn't even want them but I stole them just to steal them because I knew I could. I snuck down our thickly carpeted hallway and stood again at Alicia's door frozen by guilt and desire and confusion and lust with a raging hard-on. I raised a fist to knock but pulled away at the last second and tiptoed back to my room. I stared down the hallway from my bedroom door. Her lamp was still burning; it was the only light on under our roof and if she hadn't been there I would have been all alone in a dark house on a pitch-black night with no moon.

trump cards

at six-thirty the following morning I knocked on Alicia's door. She led me into her room but didn't close the door and stood by her dresser drying her hair with a towel. She was nude and her skin glistened with moisturizer. After she gave me a nice glimpse she threw on her robe and casually asked, "What's up?"

"You can't move out," I told her. "You're the only person who keeps Mom sane."

Alicia studied me with a neutral gaze. "Is that the only reason why you want me to stay?"

"It's a pretty good one, don't you think?"

"She's got Stuart now. She doesn't need me."

"You almost sound jealous," I said.

"Hardly."

"Why don't you get a boyfriend too. Then you guys can all hang out together."

Alicia raised her eyebrows like my suggestion amused her and replied, "You're precious. I hope you never change."

"What's that supposed to mean?"

Alicia chose not to reply and instead slid open the top drawer of her bureau and searched for something to wear. She selected a pair of lavender panties and kept looking through the drawer. She found the matching bra and untied her robe. It was clear she wasn't going to say anything.

I slammed the drawer of the bureau shut and shouted, "Why are you ignoring me!" Alicia pretended not to hear me and stepped one leg into her panties. I pushed her up against the dresser and grunted, "Answer me."

She dropped her underwear to the floor and stood there with her robe open and replied, "See now I'm confused because all this time I thought you've been asking me to ignore you."

"That's not what I'm talking about."

"Make up your mind Gator, do you want me or not?"

"I don't want you. And I don't want you to move. Mom needs you."

She smirked and replied, "How convenient."

"Not really," I said, but I had gotten a boner, which

made Alicia's smirk even bigger and that much more frustrating.

I forced her to the floor and threaded my dick though the flap of my boxers and guided it into her mouth. My knees pressed her shoulders into the dresser so she couldn't move. Her only defense was to bite but she didn't. The back of her skull made a knocking sound against the wooden doors of the bureau as I thrust in and out of her mouth. We fell to the floor and I fucked her right there against the base of the bureau with her bedroom door wide open. It was rough, angry sex and Alicia moaned loudly like I was hurting her but she clung to me and kissed my neck so I didn't stop.

When I walked out of the room she sat on the floor with her legs open wide. Her robe hung off one shoulder and her pubic hair was visible. She reached toward her ankles and pulled up her underwear as she grinned to herself.

I went to my room and took a long hot shower and got dressed for work. I grabbed Mom's pills on my way out because I was still angry and carrying them around made me feel like I was fighting back. I used to raid Mom's stash all the time, mostly for Valium, Ambien and pot. She had prescriptions for all three ever since marijuana was legalized in Boulder. Mom pretended not to notice my thefts. She'd change up her hiding spots but Alicia would tell me where to look.

Sometimes I'd get stoned in my bedroom when Mom was home. I'd stink up the second floor of the house and she wouldn't even make a peep. Fortunately Mel hated me on drugs and said I could either straighten up or lose her as my girlfriend. Mel's advice to get back at Mom was to succeed because that was the best way to show her I didn't need her. That's why I study so much and work so hard at golf now. If it weren't for Mel I'd probably be a dropout.

Mom was sitting at the kitchen table drinking coffee when I got downstairs. I didn't know she was home and worried she had heard me and Alicia upstairs. Alicia had been even louder than normal and at the time I thought her shrieks were just part of the sex play. Now I'm not so sure. She probably knew Mom was downstairs the entire time and that's why she left her bedroom door open.

I ventured a smile and cheerfully said, "Look what the cat dragged in," which sounded much crueler out loud than it had in my head. My words often sounded meaner than intended when I talked to Mom, probably because deep down I wanted to hurt her. "Sorry, that didn't come out right. I mean I'm surprised to see you since you're usually not around in the morning."

Mom stared at me silently.

"Not that I don't like seeing you. I do. But usually your bedroom door is closed which means you either want to be alone or you're down the street."

Mom's eyes narrowed.

"How is your boyfriend anyway?"

Mom's right eye twitched involuntarily, which it often did before she snapped.

"Blink once if you can hear me," I said.

She shut her eyes slowly.

"Gotcha," I said and left the house.

I rode to the club and pedaled extra hard because I was running late. Wade and I worked the bag drop most mornings and had to be there before the members arrived so we could take their bags and park their cars for them. Wade volunteered because a lot of his "clients" were members and they'd leave him cash in a designated pocket of their golf bags, which he would replace with their "orders." I worked the bag drop because it was better than hanging out in the caddy shack taking shit from everyone about Marty. Tipping wasn't allowed at the club but Lu was good about greasing all the caddies when they did stuff like that and I was trying to make as much tuition money for boarding school as possible.

When I got to the drop Mel was there talking to Wade. I wasn't worried about Wade hitting on her because even though I thought she was hot she was still a big-boned jock in everyone else's eyes and none of the guys in school were interested in dating an Amazon no matter how awesome she might be on the inside. That's one bright spot about high school; sometimes everyone is so stupid it can actually work to your advantage.

They didn't see me arrive so I took the opportunity to admire Mel from afar. She was wearing a short pink skirt and a white sleeveless top and her hair was pulled back in a ponytail. She looked girly and cute and the stretchy fabric of her skirt hugged her ass and thighs in a flattering way. A van from the fancy hotel in town with the reciprocal rights to the club arrived and eight players climbed out. Wade hopped to work and without being asked Mel helped him with the bags. One of the hotel guests slipped her some cash and she handed it to Wade when they were done, which made my heart ache even more for her.

I walked over and Wade greeted me with "It's about time, Fun Buns. Where ya been?"

"Bad hair day," I replied, and Wade gave me the finger because he knew I was busting on his mother's internet photos. "You're here early," I said to Mel, and tried to sound as upbeat as a boy who had just mock-raped his godmother could. Mel fake-smiled and started to walk away. I chased after her and she didn't stop until I grabbed her hand.

"Leave me alone," she growled, and tugged her arm loose.

"I'm sorry about last night."

"No Gates, I'm the one who's sorry. I've obviously been pressuring you to do something you really don't want to do. I probably should have picked up on this way before last night, but don't worry, I get it now, loud and clear."

She started to walk so I grabbed her hand again and said, "Mel, I've been trying to explain."

Rather than pull away she grabbed my arm and in a gentle voice said, "Actually you haven't. You've been beating around the bush about something for the past three months but you've officially lost your audience so go and not tell someone else." She spun around and off she went.

Wade watched the entire scene and asked, "What gives, Fun Buns?"

"It's complicated."

He chuckled. "It's gotta be tough when your old man has a crush on your boyfriend."

"That's not it."

"Still . . . why don't you caddy for someone else?"

"I've asked Lu a million times. He's afraid to piss off Marty."

"Fuck Marty. If Lu had any balls he'd throw him the hell out of here."

Wade's words were surprising and made me wonder if he once had a Marty or Alicia in his life. Maybe Ike and Sara suddenly quit their careers and moved from Hollywood to Boulder to give Wade a fresh start. They seemed like the type of parents who would make that sacrifice. It was nice to know good people really did exist.

"Can I ask you a question, Wade?"

"Fire away, Fun Buns."

"Why do you sell drugs? It's not like you need the money."

Wade smirked and sarcastically asked, "Does Fun Buns not approve? Are you the only guy around here who gets to make a little cash on the side?"

"Whaddaya mean?"

"Your matches for Lu. I know all about 'em and I don't buy it for a second that you're trying to raise money to pay for some phantom boarding school you're not even enrolled in. So don't flit around here like you're Mr. Clean. Besides something tells me your life is way more fucked up than mine."

"Is that so?"

"You looked in a mirror lately, Fun Buns? What are they putting in the water at your house anyway? Psycho syrup?"

"Don't talk about my mother like that."

"Then mind your business." Wade crossed his arms and looked away. I handed him the pills I stole from Mom and he read the vials and said, "Dude, these are gold."

"Sorry about the itching powder. Truce?"

Wade grinned. "You're a good man, Fun Buns. Sorry I busted on your mom."

People began to arrive right on top of each other and at one point we had a line of four cars waiting to be parked.

Just as it was quieting down, Mrs. Vanleer's white Mercedes sedan, which was always perfectly clean, rolled into sight. Wade opened the door for Mrs. Vanleer and I began to unload the bags from the trunk. As I pulled out the second bag Marty pretended to help and palmed my ass so I spun away and "accidentally" slammed the golf bag into his shin, which made him hop in pain.

Mrs. Vanleer laughed. She wore a short skirt and her shirt was really tight. She, me and Marty stood in a triangle and stared at each other and no one knew what to do or say so I carried the bags down to the pro shop because that was my job.

When Wade and I met back at the drop he said, "You must have some ass, Fun Buns, because Marty can't keep his hands off it. At least you get to stare at Mrs. Vanleer's new love bubbles for eighteen holes."

"Maybe they'll even distract Marty," I suggested optimistically.

Wade shook his head and pulled his Baggie of pills from his pocket and said, "The only way to make him stop is with a little help from my friends."

The round with the Vanleers didn't go all that bad. Mel bailed because she couldn't stand the sight of me, and Marty stayed sober and kept his distance. Mrs. Vanleer had discovered a new confidence and her rigidity had unwound. She moved fluidly and spoke with a relaxed cadence and hints of her Louisiana accent appeared in certain words and phrases. She even asked about Timmy Timmy Timmy and seemed a little bummed when I told her he was going to be gone for so long. Her golf swing and entire demeanor was carefree and loose and she shot the round of her life, an 88.

In the afternoon I got sent out for another loop with a foursome, three of whom were guests. The member was Wade's best "customer," Micky Mackanicky, and everyone called him Micky Mac. He was the founder of a shoe company that hit it big with the invention of a hideously ugly foam clog that became a fad literally around the globe. No one could believe his success because he was universally known as a moron whose best talent was catching a buzz. Micky didn't care what people thought, even after the fad passed and his company's stock crashed. He had cashed out on top and was content to play golf every day and let the haters hate. I watched Micky closely all eighteen holes and tried to figure out how he did it.

When the round was over it was late and the course was cleared out. I went to the range to practice but couldn't focus. Lu drove up in a cart. He was wearing an orange and black rugby shirt and white shorts, with an orange cable-knit sweater tied around his neck even though it was ninety degrees out. To cap it all off he had on a pair of Micky Mac's clogs . . . neon orange.

I pointed at his shoes and said, "Still wearing those, eh?"

"They're comfortable."

"You look like a candy corn that just got electrocuted."

He patted the seat of the cart and said, "Sit down. We need to talk."

"You're right," I said, "I'm not caddying for the Vanleers anymore."

"Marty's a good man."

"Maybe, but if he grabs my ass again I'm gonna snap."

Lu waved his hand and said, "Oh, he's harmless."

"Tell that to my butt cheeks."

"Marty's the man around here. If he drops his membership twenty other guys will follow and I can't afford that so make the guy happy and carry his bag."

"You carry his bag dude. I'm sick of people calling me Fun Buns."

"All the caddies worship you and you know it."

"Not anymore," I said.

"You get to use the course don't you?"

"Yeah, to make you money."

"Which you get to keep half of. Besides, don't act like you don't enjoy it. I've watched you hustle enough people to know you get off on it."

I shook my head and replied, "It's all about tuition for boarding school, my man."

"Keep telling yourself that."

"Fine. I quit. This isn't worth it."

"You might want to think about that. A guy called this morning looking for a game with you. He heard you like to play for money and wants to come down here with two of his pals for a skins match, ten grand a player. Says he's a scratch golfer but I bet he can't break eighty."

"Who is he?" I was amazed and frightened someone had actually heard about me through some twisted grapevine.

"Some rich guy from Aspen. He's probably bored out of his head and doing lines off his trophy wife's ass doesn't excite him anymore so high-stakes golf puts the lead in his pencil instead."

"That was very poetic Lu. But I still have to pass."

"I'll cover the buy-in, you keep ten percent of the winnings."

"You're fucking nuts you know that?"

Lu smirked and replied in his Confucius voice, "No. Man who stick dick in peanut butter is fucking nuts."

"And you're a racist against your own people, which is even more screwed up."

Lu swept his arm to show the expanse of the BGC and replied, "These are my people." He drove away with his orange sweater flapping in the wind.

Mom was in the kitchen when I got home. My shirt

and caddy bib were draped over my shoulder and I was covered in sweat from my ride. She stood at the counter and poured a glass of wine, which wasn't her first, judging by how much was left in the bottle. When she saw me she said, "Put your shirt on. This isn't a teen vampire movie."

I got dressed and opened the fridge to look for something to eat but then asked, "Wanna go get some dinner somewhere?"

Mom smiled like she was touched but said, "I'm going to a barbecue up Sunshine Canyon. I'd invite you but it's going to be all old people like me."

"Barbecue? I'll go."

"You really want to come?"

"Sure. You know how good a cheeseburger sounds right now? Besides, when was the last time we actually had a meal together?" And again I insulted her without trying.

Mom quickly got defensive and said, "I'm sorry I have such a busy schedule."

"I'm not trying to put you down."

"Is there something you want to say to me?"

"Like what?"

"Like why you hate me? Or how mad you are I tried to kill myself? Or how unfair it is you have a crazy mother?"

"That's not how I feel at all."

"It's how you act."

"What makes you say that?"

She laughed to herself and bitterly replied, "Nothing, angel." Her right eye began to twitch and she left the house for the night.

I ran up to Alicia's room and turned on her radio to the same loudness of her sex screams that morning. Then I ran back to the kitchen and sat in the exact spot where Mom had been sitting. The music was muffled, but I could still make out the song.

I didn't know what to do so I went to Lucky's because that's where I had good memories of me and Mel. Ike and Sara were at their regular table beneath James Dean and they smiled when I walked in the door. I waved and sat in a booth facing away from them. I ordered a cheeseburger and shake and stared at the posters of icons from a time that was surely more innocent than mine.

Alicia walked in and sat across from me. I hate to admit it but I was happy to see her. "I think Mom heard us this morning," I told her.

Alicia frowned and said, "She didn't return any of my phone calls or texts today."

"Fuck."

"What the hell came over you?"

"You pissed me off."

"You practically raped me."

My eyes darted to Ike and Sara to make sure they

couldn't hear us. "I guess that makes us even for everything that happened in Aspen then," I whispered.

"It wasn't like that and you know it so cry rape to your
erection and not me." This was the trump card she played
every time I told her our sex was against my will.

"What should we do about Mom?" I asked.

"Don't worry, if she heard us she would have killed herself by now." And this was the trump card she played to
keep me from confessing our sex to Mom. The deck was
stacked against me.

"Her eye's been twitching a lot lately. I'm kinda scared
she's gonna lose it again."

"Hey." Alicia reached across the table and grabbed my
hand. "We're in this together. I won't move out. She'll be
fine. You'll see."

We were a team, just like me and Lu doing the hustle or
when I worked the bag drop with Wade and looked the
other way while he took care of "business." My burger
came and I took a bite and slid it across the table. The waitress brought two straws with the shake and we split my
dinner and then walked home slowly in the dark.

sometimes fiction
is better than fact

*W*hen we got home it was un-
derstood we would undress together and have sex. That's
what it would take to keep Alicia in Mom's life and the
moment we got inside Alicia dragged me into Mom's room
and pushed me onto her bed. I wasn't turned on at all and
when a blow job didn't work Alicia rolled onto her back
and said, "What's the matter?"

"I don't want to do it here, it's weird." I was also distracted with thoughts about how much I loved Melanie
but I couldn't tell that to Alicia right after I'd convinced
her not to move out.

Alicia stripped down to a sexy set of black panties and
bra because she knew her lingerie was my kryptonite. She
pressed her body against mine and whispered, "Fuck me

like you hate me." I quickly got an erection and she slid me inside her and right before I orgasmed she pulled away so my cum shot all over Mom's blanket. Then she laughed and said, "Go to bed. I'll clean up."

In the morning I went to the bench in North Boulder Park and waited for the regulars but no one showed and no deer dotted the foothills. I rarely thought about my father. The last time was when I won the state high school golf championship. Mom and Alicia didn't come to the match and when the tournament host handed me the trophy no one was there to take a picture. He asked where my dad was and I told him he died in the Vietnam War, which was impossible because the war ended before I was born.

I went home and Mom and Alicia were at the kitchen table drinking coffee and reading the newspaper. I got some coffee and joined them at the table happy to be the only one in the house interested in reading the sports section. For a good long time the three of us read in silence and when I got hungry I cooked a big omelet and lots of toast for everyone. We lingered over the meal as we mocked our small town's paper for covering subjects like the plight of the prairie dog, cyclists wanting more road rights and a "scofflaw" who fled a parking ticket. These were the pressing issues in Boulder, at least the ones on public record, but obviously there's a lot more to a town than meets the eye.

We stayed in the kitchen all morning and listened to music, played cards and talked about movies. Mom did the dishes and refused help. Cleaning was her contribution to the domesticity we practiced, a rare occasion at our address, which made it that much more enjoyable. The only bad thing about the morning was it made me wonder if things would have always been that normal if I'd never slept with Alicia. Mom looked like a mother standing over the sink wearing bright yellow latex gloves and scrubbing a pan. It was probably the first time she had ever worn those gloves but the role suited her and it was a shame she couldn't have been that person all along. When Mom put the last dish in the washer she turned to me like a lightbulb had just gone off in her head and said, "Shouldn't you be at the golf course by now?" She looked at the clock on the wall; it was after noon.

"I quit," I said.

"You quit? What are you going to do all summer? You can't just sit around doing nothing."

"Why not? This morning was pretty nice, wasn't it?"

"Sure, but it's not reality." The truth of her words hung heavy in the air. She had no more dishes to clean and her hands were idle and the smile on her face dissolved as quickly as the soapsuds at the bottom of the sink. Mom said she was tired and went to her room to lie down.

Alicia said to me, "Thanks for ruining a perfectly good morning," and ran after Mom.

I waited around for a while to see if they'd come back. Mom's bedroom door was closed and the faint smell of marijuana seeped out into the living room from beneath her door along with the muffled sound of giggles.

So I hit the road to Harmony's Rest. I wasn't due to read to the group until much later that day but Harmony's Rest was my favorite hideout and Cliff was like a grandfather and always up to talk or share a bench in silence. The home has a small indoor pool for low-impact water aerobics but mostly it's just a hangout for visiting grandkids. The poolroom was Cliff's favorite spot in the building. He never went in the water but liked the unpredictable shrieks of the toddlers. He said the sound of play echoing off the water through the chlorine-thickened air was like "television for the blind."

I found Cliff near the pool. Splash marks dampened the cuffs of his pants. He was pleased by my unexpected arrival and asked, "Is it five o'clock already?"

"I'm a few hours early." I grabbed his hand to give him my bearing.

"Did you bring a new book?"

"I did. It's about a soldier in Vietnam who goes AWOL and hikes to Paris to find his lover."

Cliff nodded. "That was a nasty war."

"I know. Sometimes I pretend my dad died there."

Cliff stood and steadied himself on my shoulder. "Come on," he said with a trace of tough love in his voice.

I followed him to the chapel. Normally we'd sit on a bench beneath a big old cottonwood but it was too hot outside and the chapel was the coolest room on-site because the floors were stone, the ceilings vaulted and the stained glass windows tempered the sunlight. I wasn't planning on downloading on Cliff but he loved a good story, happy or sad, and listened carefully as I told him everything about Mom and how I had never met my father.

"What was his name?" Cliff asked.

"I don't know. I don't know my father's name."

Someone played an organ from a small balcony at the front of the chapel and I shut my eyes and tried to hear the same music as Cliff. Just as the song was reaching the climax the organist stumbled and botched a note. Cliff grabbed my forearm and whispered, "Bollocks." He kept his hand on my arm for the remainder of the song.

Going After Cacciato, the new book I smuggled in, was a hit and as a group we agreed that what Phyllis didn't know wouldn't hurt her. I read about the Vietnam War for two hours to a wide-eyed audience. I liked reading about that war because even though my father was never there I pretended it was his leaping on a live grenade to save his unit that kept him from me. Sometimes fiction is better than fact.

When I got home the house was empty and there was no note from Mom or Alicia; they never left word. I envied those kids whose parents cared enough to leave a message explaining where they were and what they were doing and when they'd be back and that yes they were still alive. In my house you never really knew. There was beer in the fridge so I cracked one open. I try not to drink because the doctor told me boozing's a bad idea thanks to the awesome genes Mom passed on to me. Last year at a party I drank so much I ended up in the ER with alcohol poisoning. Alicia came and got me in the middle of the night because Mom was away on one of her last-minute vacations. Alicia's penalty for my drunkenness was to ground me in the house for four days of sex. At the time I didn't see how the punishment fit the crime. Now I understand she was punishing Mom.

The doorbell rang and it was Melanie looking pretty as ever. Her hair was wet and she wore a sleeveless, greenish-colored dress that buttoned up her back and stopped just above her knees. On her feet were preppy bright sandals. Mel was a jeans and T-shirt kind of girl (another reason to love her) but the fancy clothes suited her well. "You look nice," I said. "Why you all dressed up?"

That got a smile and she cheekily replied, "Thanks, I have a date."

"Lucky guy." I tugged her dress and said, "That's an interesting color. Whaddaya call it?"

Mel lifted up the hem and inspected the fabric and replied, "Sea foam I think. Mom picked it out. It was sitting on my bed for me one day when I got home from school, but of course the dress was two sizes too small so I had to get it exchanged." She smirked and sarcastically added, "Mom's a subtle one."

"Well I'd say sea foam looks good on you but it doesn't really sound all that flattering."

"Tell me anyway."

"Sea foam looks good on you." It got that weird kind of quiet. "I'm sorry about everything," I said.

Mel was about to sit on the front step but remembered she was dressed up and remained standing. She smoothed the front of her dress and said, "I really don't want us to break up, but if you're not attracted to me just tell me and I promise I won't be upset with you and we can still be friends."

"Mel, I think you're beautiful. Every time I'm with you I find a new reason to love you."

"Tell me one now."

"Okay." I thought for a second. "You don't even know the color of your dress. I love that about you."

She smiled and said, "Something's wrong Gator."

I took a sip of beer and replied, "I know. I've been trying to tell you something but sometimes it seems like you don't want to hear it."

"Of course I want to hear it."

"You've stopped me a bunch of times."

Her face grew stern. "Maybe you haven't noticed but my parents are getting stranger and stranger by the day."

"I've definitely noticed."

"So it's stressing me out and I want to have some fun rather than studying while we're on a date or spending all our free time practicing golf, or getting all caught up in serious talks."

"I had no idea I was such a bore."

Mel grabbed the beer bottle, took a swig and passed it back. "Well now you know." She crossed her arms because she knew she was being a bitch but was determined to hold her ground. I actually loved her for that.

"Whatever, Mel. Go have fun on your date."

"It's not a date. It's a stupid fund-raiser for the police that Mom's hosting and she's making me go."

"Well la-dee-da."

"Hey, if you have something to say then spit it out already."

"It's not something you just spit out. Jesus, Mel. Forget it, alright?"

"Sorry," Mel said sincerely. "But maybe if you didn't act like my mouth tastes like sour milk every time we kiss I wouldn't be so afraid of what you're going to tell me."

I pulled her in close and gave her my absolute best kiss. "Your mouth tastes awesome," I told her. "Go have fun tonight." I slipped inside and locked the door. Mel stood on the steps for a full minute before she left. She didn't ring the doorbell or knock on the door or anything. She was just savoring the moment. Mel was always doing dorky things like that and it never embarrassed her. Just another reason to love her.

Mom and Alicia pulled into the driveway while I was in the kitchen getting another beer and I didn't want them to see me drinking so I hid in the staircase off the kitchen that leads to the basement. They walked inside with their arms loaded with boxes from the liquor store topped with bags of ice and sleeves of big red plastic cups. They quickly set about unpacking the booze and mixers.

"What time did you invite people over?" Mom asked Alicia.

Alicia looked at her watch and replied, "About an hour from now."

"Gates is going to be pissed when he comes home to a party."

"Well any normal kid would be thrilled."

Mom laughed. "He's not normal, that's for sure."

"Have you told him about this weekend yet?" She hadn't but I already knew they were going away. The Food & Wine Festival was that weekend in Aspen and Mom and Alicia went every year; so did Melanie and her parents and about half the town of Boulder. It was kind of a thing.

Mom replied, "Gates won't come to Aspen with us and I shouldn't leave him here alone."

"If he's not working he should do whatever you tell him."

"You know how much he hates Aspen," Mom replied. The room got silent until Mom said, "I doubt he'll ever forgive me."

Alicia casually unpacked lemons from a brown paper bag and replied, "Don't be too hard on yourself."

"I think he masturbated on my bed last night."

Alicia dropped the bag of lemons to the floor and said, "Excuse me?"

Mom nodded. "What do you think I should say to him? You're the expert."

Alicia laughed and said, "I don't know about that one . . . tell him to be more careful I guess."

They shared a good laugh and then Mom said, "Hopefully at some point we can all just move on because right now it feels like he really hates me."

I couldn't believe what I was hearing. I threw a silent punch at the wall and noticed little lines marked with dates delineating my height and age through the years. The records stopped the year I went to Aspen.

"I don't think he hates you at all," Alicia said.

"Then why would he tell Stuart I lived in a mental home?"

I had never spoken to Stuart in my life! I inched closer to the crack in the door.

"Maybe it wasn't Gates," Alicia said.

"Who else would leave a note in his mailbox? No one even knows we're dating. Let me tell ya, men don't really like it when they find out their girlfriend was locked in a padded room."

Alicia waved it off. "Wait until Stuart sees all the cars parked outside the house tonight. He'll know you're having a party and will get so jealous he'll walk right on over and beg you to take him back."

"I'd still like to know who sent him that letter," Mom said.

"Forget about it. Just have a good time tonight and let's look forward to a fun weekend in Aspen together, with or without Gates. He can take care of himself for a few days if he has to." Alicia held out her arms and they hugged. "Everything is going to be fine, okay?"

Mom nodded and Alicia leaned in and kissed her on the lips. They didn't make out but it was more than just a friendly kiss. Mom bowed her head and Alicia lifted her chin and kissed her softly on the mouth again. Mom backed away and made herself busy on the other side of the kitchen but Alicia followed and said, "Hey, you're beautiful and everyone knows it, especially Stuart."

"Thanks for being so great," Mom said. "I don't know why you put up with me."

Alicia pulled Mom in for another kiss. Mom had her

hands on Alicia's shoulders like she was ready to push her away but she opened her mouth and kissed Alicia back. Then they broke into laughter. I had a pencil from the BGC and marked my height and the date and walked into the kitchen and said, "Knock, knock."

Mom smiled and asked, "Where'd you come from?"

"I was looking for an old club in the basement. Which reminds me, do you remember how much you paid for that putter you bought at the garage sale?"

Mom raised her eyebrows and in a bit of a snobby tone replied, "Garage sale? I've never bought anything in my life at a garage sale." She looked at Alicia and chuckled.

Alicia tried to act natural but I could tell she knew I'd caught Mom in a lie. To change the subject she said, "We're going to Aspen this weekend and if you don't have a job you're coming with us." I'd rather caddy for Marty a hundred times than go back to Aspen. Even knowing Mel would be there the same weekend wasn't enough to make the trip appealing.

"Ah, Memory Lane," I said. "That'd be quite a threesome." I smirked at them both. Mom's eye began to twitch. I pointed at all the booze and said, "Party on, girls," and walked out of the house.

I wanted to have a long dinner at Lucky's but Lu and Wade were eating there together, which was very odd, so I went to the movies. The party was still in full swing when I got home but I snuck in a basement window and headed upstairs without being seen. The place reeked of cigarettes and dope. I peeked in the kitchen on my way up the back staircase and saw Mom sitting on the kitchen counter with her skirt hitched above her waist. A man was kneeling on the floor in front of her, I think it was Stuart but his head was between her legs so I couldn't make a proper ID. That's a vision I'll live with for the rest of my life but even more disturbing was the sight of Alicia standing behind the man, masturbating as she watched.

Around two in the morning, once it was finally quiet, Alicia came to my room dressed in black stockings and garters. She carried a candle and put it on my bedside table.

"Go away," I said.

"Oh, don't be such a tough guy." She sat on the bed and pulled down the sheets. "Your mother left with Stuart an hour ago. I thought you'd be happy to know her spirits are high again."

"Why'd you break them up just to get them back together again?"

"Why do you think I broke them up?"

"I saw you guys in the kitchen this afternoon. I didn't leave any note about Mom in Stuart's mailbox so it must have been you. I also saw you kiss her," I said.

Alicia slid beneath the sheets and climbed on top of me so her tits were in my face. "I've been a bad bad girl.

Punish me." Her breath reeked of alcohol and she was uncharacteristically drunk so something about the party must have stressed her out.

I didn't have a boner and nothing was stirring down below. "I saw you guys in the kitchen tonight too," I said.

"Saw what?"

"The three of you."

"Spying on your mother's sex life is perverted. You should be ashamed of yourself."

"Looked like you were doing more than just spying," I said.

Alicia snickered and grabbed my penis but I was as limp as a wet noodle.

"Sorry," I said without a hint of regret. "I'm in love with Melanie."

"You're only seventeen years old. You don't even know what love is."

"Maybe, but I know what love isn't, and that's this."

Alicia groaned and rolled over and passed out. For the first time in a long time I was actually proud of myself. All I could think about was Melanie and how I wished I could explain that loving her was the greatest reason of all to love her.

a bridge too far

I slipped out of bed at six in the morning and Alicia was still out cold. The living room was wrecked. Red plastic cups pocked the area and I gathered them slowly. A cherry red press-on nail floated in one glass; cigarette butts and lime wedges were sunk in others. A lone flip-flop was abandoned beneath the couch, a credit card was forgotten on the smudged glass top of the coffee table, along with an orange lighter, a half pack of Parliament Lights and a boarding pass for a plane ticket from Sioux Falls to Denver with the passenger listed as Patrick Caruso. I had never heard of Patrick Caruso and was pretty certain throwing out his boarding pass would be the closest we'd ever come to meeting.

I was carrying a bottle of vodka to the kitchen when

the doorbell rang and I answered in my boxers with the bottle in my hand. The last person I expected to see was Melanie but there she was wearing a long trench coat even though the sun was rising and the day was already warm.

She looked at the bottle in my hand and said, "I see you switched to the hard stuff."

I smiled and explained, "Mom threw a party last night to make her boyfriend jealous and win him back. She didn't sleep at home last night so the plan worked but now the place is trashed."

Mel shook her head and laughed.

"And . . . ," I added, "I'm pretty sure they were doing coke on the coffee table in the living room. Was anyone doing lines at your mom's party?"

"Well the place was filled with cops and politicians so yeah they probably were."

I laughed. "Boulder cops may not be able to catch a criminal but they sure know how to catch a buzz."

"I think my parents are getting divorced," Mel said. "Mom threw herself at every cop she talked to last night and Dad didn't even come home with us. When I snuck out this morning they were fighting in the kitchen. Dad was still wearing his tux and Mom had her gown from last night on. They were both up drinking all night."

"What were they fighting about?"

"I don't know." Melanie knew what the fight was about but didn't want to tell me. The girl couldn't lie to save her life, another reason to love her. Her eyes twinkled like she had been given a dare and she opened her coat to reveal an outfit of nothing but a pink set of satin lingerie. She'd spent the first few days of summer vacation lying in the sun and her skin was already tan. Her body looked great. She was shedding her baby fat daily and becoming toned. She had never looked more beautiful. Mel arched an eyebrow and brushed past me into the house and said, "Come on, let's go to your room."

My godmother was in that very room also dressed in lingerie. I chased after Mel and blocked the stairs. "So how was your date?"

"Boring." She pushed toward the stairs but I didn't budge.

"Wait," I said. "Did you really bring someone?"

"No, but they sat me next to some guy who just got home from college and he was a total dweeb. He kept making all these creepy jokes about how I could get him arrested."

"If you needed a dinner partner why didn't you ask me?"

"Because you would have had to wear a jacket and tie and I knew you wouldn't want to go." She tugged my hand and said, "Come on, move."

"You don't think I'm good enough for your mom's fancy parties, do you?"

Mel dropped my hand and sighed. "I'm really glad I came over. This is working out just as I planned." She slumped into a chair and her coat flapped open but she didn't bother to fix it.

I hated being a prick but the alternative was worse. "What exactly were you planning anyway? Do you think my house is such a free-for-all you can show up in your underwear and my mom won't even care because she's some kind of nut job?"

Mel wasn't about to back down. Another reason to love her. She made a big sarcastic show of looking around the room and said, "Well I don't see her anywhere do you?" Then she gestured toward the credit card and the smudged white residue on the coffee table and asked, "Want some blow?"

"Whatever, you're totally missing the point."

"The point is you're picking a fight with me while I'm throwing myself at you and that sucks."

Alicia appeared at the top of the staircase wearing a white sheer robe over her black underwear and garters from the night before. I cleared my throat to catch her attention and when she saw us she grinned because despite being two decades older than Melanie she still looked sexier than her in lingerie. "A little early for a playdate don't you think?" she said, staring at Mel.

Mel quickly sat up and closed her coat. She looked at me and whispered, "Does she realize she's practically naked?"

I shouted to Alicia, "Go back to bed, it's early."

Alicia came downstairs and stood in front of Mel. "What a gorgeous, healthy girl." *Healthy* was a substitute for *fat*. We all knew it.

Mel turned to me and said, "I'm gonna go now."

"You don't have to go," Alicia said and walked back upstairs.

Mel was rattled. "Does she always walk around like that? Wade said he was here once and she was waltzing around practically naked."

"I know. She didn't know he was here."

"Does she do that a lot?"

"Kinda."

"Well don't you think that's weird? What does your mom say about that?"

"She doesn't do it when Mom's here."

"Just when you're alone, huh?" Mel stood up and asked, "Why are you telling me this? If you want to break up with me at least have the balls to say it."

"I don't want to break up with you."

She looked around the trashed living room. "This was such a bad idea."

I was still holding the bottle of vodka. I took a swig and said, "Let's go to my room."

"I'm going home."

"Why?"

"Don't pretend like you're disappointed. You can't act for shit." She walked out the door and all I could do was add up the reasons to love her.

Alicia came downstairs after Mel left and leaned against the banister like some kind of lingerie model. "That was awkward," she said with a grin.

"You should have stayed upstairs."

"I didn't know she was here. It's six in the morning."

"You wanted to spook her. Mission accomplished." I sat on the couch and rested the bottle of vodka in my lap.

Alicia seated herself next to me and took the bottle out of my lap and placed it by the credit card on the coffee table. Then she stared at me and tried to tell me something with her eyes.

"What?" I said.

"You're changing."

"I know. Please don't stop me."

"We've been through a lot together, haven't we?"

"Did you know I was watching when you kissed Mom?"

"No."

"Then why'd you do it?"

Alicia looked at the front door and said, "She could come home any second. What do you think she'd say if she saw us here on the couch in our underwear like this?" I didn't answer so Alicia guessed, "Probably nothing."

"That's what kills me," I replied.

Alicia could tell I was weakening. She moved in to kiss me but I stopped her. "Suit yourself," she said, and sauntered up the stairs.

It was another moment to feel proud but Alicia had a special scent early in the mornings that always made me hard. I didn't follow her and she didn't even know I'd gotten aroused but I was still disheartened because even though I was changing for the better it felt like a bridge too far to cross. The abandoned credit card and the bottle of vodka sat on the table in front of me. The edges of the credit card were caked with white powder, which I licked clean. There was more white residue on the table so I wiped it up with my finger and licked that too. Then I took a long swig of booze and lit up a Parliament.

After the butt and more vodka I threw on some clothes and headed off to the BGC with a six-pack of beer and the rest of the smokes. I steered my bike with one hand and held a cigarette and a beer with the other. It was early in the morning and the other cyclists were too caught up in themselves to care about a drunk teenager pedaling down the road but I did get a few dirty looks for my second-hand smoke. I finished the first beer and heaved the empty bottle at a DEER CROSSING sign. A dump truck spewing a thin wisp of dust from beneath the tarp of its cargo bed headed toward me and I almost intentionally swerved into its path but the driver had done nothing wrong and his life would've been changed forever and that didn't seem fair.

When I got to the course only the groundskeepers were there, rolling the greens and mowing the fairways. I had five beers to plow through and used the key Lu hid in the cart shed to let myself into the pro shop so I could drink alone in the stockroom but Lu was there asleep on an inflatable mattress. He had a blanket and pillow and had even set up a little reading lamp. He was startled to see me and sat up quickly and rubbed his eyes. "What are you doing here?" he asked and looked at his watch. "Is that a beer?"

I took a huge gulp. "If you're gonna make me caddy for Marty I ain't doing it sober. You sleeping here now?"

Lu stretched his arms into the air and yawned. "I'm putting a steam shower in my master bath and the plumbing's shut off." In his Confucius voice he added, "And house with no bathroom is uncanny."

"You need to stop lying, especially if you want my help." I downed the rest of my beer and popped open the third. "Mind if I smoke here?" I lit up before he answered.

Lu swatted at the smoke in the air. "I talked to my guy

at the St. Julien. He said you took a grand off the boys from Omaha."

"Maybe, maybe not." I took a deep drag and coughed.

Lu got out of bed. He had slept in capri pajama pants with windmills embroidered all over them and a Harvard T-shirt. He regarded me quizzically and asked, "Did you fall and hit your head or something?"

"Harvard, eh?" I smirked. "Makes you look smart. Unfortunately the windmills on your pants make you look dumb so the outfit's pretty much a wash." I took a tug on my brew.

Lu didn't appreciate my joke. "You screwed me out of five hundred bucks."

I shrugged and drank more beer.

"I thought we were partners," he said.

"Then stop making me do things I don't want to do, like caddy for Marty." I finished the beer and opened another.

"I want my money," Lu said.

"Spent it all on beer." I held up the bottle by its neck with two fingers.

"That's okay. You can make it up when you play the guy from Aspen."

I shook my head. "Don't bother. I won't even show up."

Lu furrowed his brow. "I don't like this new attitude."

"Do you take me seriously, Lu?"

Lu grabbed a towel and some toiletries from a duffel bag and said, "I take anyone who owes me money seriously." Then he left for the shower.

The stockroom smelled like Sleeping Lu so I drank the final beer in the caddy shack. I was good and drunk by the time Wade arrived at the bag drop and parking the members' cars that morning was extra fun. During a lull I asked Wade why he told Melanie about seeing Alicia in her underwear and he replied, "I dunno, I thought it was funny."

"Like funny weird or funny ha-ha?"

"Both I guess."

"But you thought she was hot, remember?"

Wade looked at me sideways and asked, "How many beers have you had?" After some thoughtful deliberation he said, "Your godmother's face is kinda squished up and she looks like she always smells a fart but she does have some pretty sweet rib cushions."

"Would you bang her?"

He chuckled and said, "Okay, now you really are being weird. I don't think I've ever seen you this drunk before, Fun Buns. I like it." The Vanleers pulled into the parking lot and Wade said, "Your boyfriend's here."

Marty climbed out of the passenger seat and in a southern accent said, "Bring out the gimp." He burst into a fit of laughter and told me to get two Bloody Marys and meet them on the range. Mrs. Vanleer had been driving but she was as hammered as Marty. She had vamped herself up with lipstick, a tight sleeveless shirt to show off her new twins and a blue and white checked skirt she must have hemmed because it barely covered her thighs. She wore that skirt all the time and originally the fabric draped below her knees. She tried to toss the car keys to me but they sailed over my head.

Wade parked their car and I took their bags down to the pro shop and loaded them onto a cart because they were in no shape to walk. I got their drinks from the bar and met Wade back at the drop.

"It's time for a little help from your friends," I told him.

Wade said it all with his smile. He used a golf ball to crush a yellow pill inside a scorecard and stirred it slowly into the drinks. "This is ketamine," he explained. "It's a tranquilizer, which Marty obviously needs when he's around your perky fun buns. And just so she doesn't feel left out we'll dump a little bit in Silicone Sally's drink too. Now what about you compadre? You want a little ecstasy to keep that buzz rollin'?"

I shut my eyes and opened wide and Wade popped the pill down my throat and said, "Don't do anything I wouldn't do, Fun Buns."

But I had already crossed that bridge.

le big mac

*t*he club was packed. All the members had decided to come out and play and half of them brought guests. Micky Mac was holding court at the near end of the range. He always had a crowd and they drank and marked their territory with clouds of cigar smoke whether it was Saturday afternoon or Tuesday morning. The Vanleers were at the far side of the range, warming up slowly. They blended in with the other members and looked so innocent I got second thoughts about my plan. A garbage can was halfway between me and the Vanleers and I was going to dump their drinks but laughter erupted from Micky Mac's entourage and Mrs. Vanleer looked over just as I got to the trash so I had to hold on to the cups and put them in the cart.

Marty was hitting little chip shots with a wedge and didn't look up when I arrived. Most of the people on the range had been to Mrs. Vanleer's fund-raiser the night before and stole glances our way. I stood a few feet behind the Vanleers with a wet towel draped over the shoulder of my caddy bib and waited to clean their clubs. They were the king and queen of Boulder and I was the fly on their crumbling walls. Marty hadn't played a sober round of golf in months and Mrs. Vanleer was dressing like a teenager to show off her new body. Such things don't go unnoticed. People were talking and it didn't matter how many galas Mrs. Vanleer hosted, the rumors were getting louder. Maybe that's why she showed up to the club drunk that morning.

The course was jammed but we were only a twosome so we went off the back nine first since it was empty. The tenth tee is set off to the east of the pro shop, well out of sight of the clubhouse's large balcony. It's a two-minute ride from the range to the tee box and the three of us squeezed into the cart and I drove. Marty hadn't spoken a word all morning and kept his hands to himself even though we were practically sitting in each other's laps. Driving the cart made me realize just how wasted I was. My fingers tingled and then my hands turned to rubber. When the breeze blew I felt every hair on my head move. The ice jiggling in the Vanleers' drinks looked like a kaleidoscope.

When we got to the tee I grabbed both Bloody Marys and walked them to the garbage can. Mrs. Vanleer ran after me and grabbed the cups but I didn't let go. "I think you guys are all set," I said. "How much have you had to drink anyway?"

Mrs. Vanleer's eyes twinkled and she said, "Just a bottle of champagne . . . each."

Marty rested his head on the steering wheel. "He doesn't look so hot."

"Marty didn't come home until breakfast so I can't speak for how he's feeling. But he's a big boy and soon enough he's going to want his Bloody Mary and as we all know, Marty gets what Marty wants." She tugged the drinks free and carried them back to the cart. Then she swatted Marty on the head and said, "You're up, Tiger."

Marty climbed out of the cart and grabbed his driver from me without speaking. "Make sure you keep it down the left side," I said, and he laughed so hard he nearly coughed up a lung. But then he teed up his ball and miraculously hit a long one down the left edge of the fairway.

Mrs. Vanleer wasn't as adept at golfing while impaired and popped her drive forty feet in the air but only twenty feet forward. She ran after her ball like a little girl chasing a butterfly and teed it up in the fairway. With a slow half swing she bunted a shot about twenty-five yards and chased it again. For the first two holes Marty crookedly drove the cart alongside Mrs. Vanleer as she prodded her ball little by little around the course. Neither of them touched their drinks and Marty played well for being out all night. He and Mrs. Vanleer ignored each other and he didn't speak to me once. He kept his hands to himself and the morning streamed by calmly.

Beauty was everywhere. When birds flew overhead their flapping wings played a symphony. Branches of trees bent into the sky like sculptures. The sweet smell of cut grass lingered in the breeze. On the eleventh green I decided to throw out both drinks at the twelfth tee when no one was looking but when I got to the cart both cups were empty. The Vanleers must have chugged them while I raked a sand trap Mrs. Vanleer demolished when she took ten swings to try and hit out from it.

The twelfth hole is a long par 3 that plays northwest to an undulated green well guarded by sand traps. The men's tee is elevated away from the seniors' and ladies' tee and the only access is a steep set of stairs leading to a panoramic view of the foothills and Left Hand Canyon. When we got to the top of the stairs, far away from Mrs. Vanleer, Marty turned to me and whispered, "Gates? Have you ever given a foot massage?" He stepped aside to let me pass and palmed my ass. We both checked to see if Mrs. Vanleer was watching but she was squatting behind a small pine tree taking a leak.

By the time we reached the fourteenth green the sun was high and hot and Marty called the clubhouse to have "one of the gal's" drive out four more Bloodys. We waited on the fifteenth tee box for the drinks to arrive and all three of us sat in the cart to stay out of the sun. I was sandwiched between them and Marty reclined with his feet on the dashboard and his head hanging off the back of the seat. His eyes were closed and he mumbled about a five-dollar milk shake. Mrs. Vanleer's knee pressed against mine. Sweat gathered between our knees and she moved her leg up and down against mine in tiny increments, which I pretended not to notice. She closed her eyes and breathed slowly through her nose. The sound of her breath was oceanic and soothing so I closed my eyes and joined her. Mrs. Vanleer pressed her knee harder and harder against me and leaned into my shoulder. Marty snored at our pace. We were all in such a trance we didn't even hear Pam, the "gal" from the clubhouse, arrive.

Pam coughed to get our attention and my eyes popped open. Mrs. Vanleer and Marty stayed in their trance. I raised my finger to my lips and carefully climbed out of the cart. When I got to Pam she whispered, "What the hell are you guys doing?"

"They're meditating," I said quietly. "I'm walking them through a relaxation technique where they visualize their shots."

"Mr. Vanleer looks like he's asleep. How much have they had to drink?"

"He's fine."

"He doesn't look fine. And why was Mrs. Vanleer sitting in your lap?" Pam had just graduated from the University of Colorado and was starting law school in the fall. She was constantly blowing smoke up Marty's ass and stalked him at the club because he was the most powerful lawyer in town. Pam eyed me distrustfully and said, "What would Melanie say if I told her you and her mom were all over each other?"

"She'd probably think you were pathetic because she knows how desperate you are to get a job with her dad."

Pam thought she was better than everyone else who worked at the club because she was going to be a lawyer. She was constantly putting down her waitressing job in front of the other waitstaff. Pam snickered, "Desperate is getting your girlfriend's mother drunk so you can hit on her."

"Mr. and Mrs. Vanleer!" I shouted so they'd open their eyes. "Pam here thinks you've been overserved and doesn't want to give you your drinks."

Marty scowled at her and said, "I'm American, honey."

Pam ran to their cart with their drinks and quickly placed them in the cup holders. "Actually," Pam said apologetically, "I was asking Gates if he thought you guys needed anything else?"

Marty closed his eyes and leaned his head back. Mrs. Vanleer smiled at Pam and replied, "We've got everything we need right here," and patted Marty's leg tenderly.

Before she drove off Pam gave me the old stink eye and said, "*Meditating*," under her breath like it was the most ridiculous explanation in the world.

Mrs. Vanleer very generously offered me a drink and before we reached the next green all the booze was gone. Marty consumed two of the four cups and was too demolished to golf. Mrs. Vanleer hit three balls in a row into the pond in front of the fifteenth green, which she usually had no problem clearing.

"Maybe we should pack it in," I suggested.

"I don't want to stop," she said.

We skipped to the sixteenth tee and she killed a drive down the middle of the fairway. She spun around while her ball was still in the air and exclaimed, "Ha! My eyes weren't even open! Maybe I should do everything with my eyes closed!" She looked at me; my arm was wrapped around Marty to keep him from oozing out of the cart and she frowned.

Marty tried to lift his head and speak but his entire body had gone slack. Then he wet his pants and laughed and said, "Well, we'd have to be talkin' about one charmin' motherfuckin' pig."

I sped the cart back toward the fifteenth green and took

the dirt maintenance road along the perimeter of the club's property to get back to the parking lot without driving past the clubhouse. Frostbite manned the bag drop while he talked to Pam. I humped Marty over my shoulder and poured him into the backseat of his car. Mrs. Vanleer stumbled into the front passenger seat as I loaded their clubs in the trunk. Then I drove the cart to the bag drop.

Frostbite and Pam hadn't taken their eyes off us from the moment we drove into the parking lot. I stopped the cart softly and smiled like everything was cool and said, "Will you bring the cart down for me, Frostbite? Mr. Vanleer just chugged four Bloody Marys and now he can hardly walk. Mrs. Vanleer's about to have a nervous breakdown she's so embarrassed."

Frostbite looked at me funny and said, "Since when do you meditate, Fun Buns?"

Pam stared along skeptically.

"Since forever," I answered. "Why do you think I always win?" It was a lame, cocky comment but I was blitzed and I do and say the dumbest things when I'm wasted. Frostbite and Pam rolled their eyes and shook their heads but neither of them said anything back so at least I shut them up.

I was in no shape to drive but this was officially an emergency. The BGC is five miles north of town and surrounded by what used to be farms but are now just fancy homes. The terrain is flat and popular with cyclists who wear bright spandex outfits and ride in packs like swarms of homoerotic bees. I slowly drove away from the club and had to concentrate to keep a straight line. A mile into the journey a police barricade was erected because one of the road's two lanes had been shut to make room for a triathlon. A cop was directing traffic but when it was our turn he held up his hand and halted us.

Marty felt the car stop and sat up to look out the window. I watched him in the rearview mirror try to open the door so I quickly hit the automatic locks. He didn't like being trapped and banged on the window, which caught the policeman's attention. The cop started walking toward us and I muttered, "Oh shit . . ."

Mrs. Vanleer rolled down her window and waved. In a flirty voice I'd never heard her use she purred, "Hello, Officer Chase . . ." The cop recognized her and stopped all the other traffic so he could signal us through.

I got us off the main road at the first opportunity and took a meandering route through side streets and quiet neighborhoods to get to the Vanleers' house. When we reached the driveway Mrs. Vanleer and I looked at Marty, who lay sideways in the backseat, and she asked, "So what's next?"

I carried Marty inside and lay him down in his study, a wood-paneled den decorated with leather couches, framed law degrees, and college football paraphernalia from the good old days. Mrs. Vanleer shut all the blinds and Marty restarted the DVD player, in which *Pulp Fiction* had been paused. He tried to recite the dialogue along with the actors but was too groggy to keep up. A fancy bottle of bourbon and two bar glasses were set on a tray atop his desk. I poured a tall drink and took a healthy sip, then Mrs. Vanleer polished it off and said, "I'm gonna get something smoother."

I was still wearing my caddy bib so I took it off and tried to drape it over the back of the couch but it fell to the floor. I needed to have a talk with Marty and thought he'd take me more seriously if I wasn't wearing my caddy uniform. He was holding the remote so I took it from him and paused the movie. He looked at me with droopy eyes and gurgled, "Le Big Mac."

Firmly I said, "Why do you think it's okay to keep grabbing my ass even though I've asked you a million times to stop?"

He was lying on his back and he sat up and looked right at me. I was expecting him to say something like *Bacon tastes gooood, pork chops taste gooood,* but instead he said, "I bet it happens to you a lot. You know why? Because you're a born victim. It's written all over your eyes." He plucked the controls from my fingers and continued the movie.

I felt like I had reached the end of a bridge but was only

halfway across the river. I grabbed the smokes from my pocket and lit one up. The manly room was cigar friendly and provided a thick crystal ashtray on the coffee table along with a silver Zippo lighter. Mrs. Vanleer returned with a tray of cold Mexican beers, a bottle of tequila, a saltshaker and a plate of lemon wedges. She perked up at the sight of me smoking and said, "This day just keeps getting better."

There were two leather couches set in an L formation. Marty was laid out on one and Mrs. Vanleer and I sat on the other. The scene on the TV was the foot massage exchange Marty was so fond of and the three of us watched in silence. Mrs. Vanleer and I did a few shots of tequila and she lit a cigarette with the grace, familiarity and glee of a closet smoker. She slipped off her sandals and swung her feet into my lap so I quickly hopped up and excused myself to the bathroom.

I hung out in the kitchen and drank two more beers and by the time I got back to the den they were out cold. Marty had rolled onto his side and looked like he had stopped breathing. Mrs. Vanleer lay flat on her back with her legs splayed open. She had pulled her skirt up over her waist. Her underwear dangled off one ankle and her hand hung limp inside her thigh. I should have run but instead did another shot of tequila and lit up a cigarette. Then Mel's car pulled into the driveway. The movie had ended and the TV cast a blue haze through the smoke across the room. Melanie's car alarm beeped to signal the doors were locked. I only had a few seconds but I took another drag of my cigarette, exhaled slowly and wondered how a person can change what's written in their eyes.

the kennebunkport
picnic police

*t*here was no way out of the house without crossing Mel's path and the only place to hide was beneath Marty's enormous wooden desk. I kicked my caddy bib under the couch while scampering to get out of sight. I should have just grabbed it then but I was wasted and not thinking clearly. The room was dark because the blinds were down and there was a small crack in the desk's antique wood that served as an excellent peephole. The coffee table was littered with cigarettes, booze and two shot glasses. The scene was very similar to the state of Mom's living room that same morning where my trip began and passenger Caruso's had ended.

Mel came through the front door and called for her parents. Being balled up beneath a piece of furniture made me nauseous. The air in the room was smoky and layered with Marty's gas and Mrs. Vanleer's sex. Mel opened the door and said, "You guys in here?" She sniffed, wrinkled her forehead and tilted her head like a bewildered puppy. "Mom? Dad? Have you guys been smoking? It stinks in here." Her eyes scanned the tequila, the beers, the shot glasses. The back of Mrs. Vanleer's couch must have blocked Mel's view of her mother's exposed crotch because Mel was more concerned about Marty and rushed to his side. She nudged his legs but he didn't stir. "Dad?" There was no reply so she pushed him harder. "Dad! Wake up!"

Marty groaned like a dying sea lion. He rolled over and fell off the couch and knocked Mel to the floor with him. He blew air through his lips so they flapped like a horse's and punctuated the sigh with a similar-sounding fart. Mel looked at her mom and froze when she saw her state of undress. She hopped over to Mrs. Vanleer's couch and gently pulled her skirt down. Mrs. Vanleer lifted her head a couple of inches to peer at her daughter, then she lay back and said, "Go back to bed honey, it's late."

"It's two in the afternoon."

Mrs. Vanleer rolled over and fell back asleep and Melanie stormed out and a minute later her car left the driveway. I waited to make sure she wasn't coming back and to give Marty and Mrs. Vanleer time to drift to their happy places. I was nervous and drunk and claustrophobic and needed to talk to someone so I called Timmy Timmy Timmy. He'd been gone for less than three days but I missed him.

He answered, "Gator Gator, violator."

I whispered, "Timmy Timmy Timmy."

"Hello hello hello? Gates, is that you you you?"

"Sorry, I gotta whisper."

"Are you okay okay okay?"

"No. I'm kinda wasted right now."

"It's the middle of the day day day."

"I almost killed Mr. Vanleer."

"Dude, why are you drunk drunk drunk? You know you shouldn't drink drink drink." Well that just tickled me silly and as hard as I tried not to laugh at 3T's tic, I couldn't. Timmy Timmy Timmy hung up, as he should have. I called him back three times but he wouldn't answer. I felt so badly about myself I wanted to die, then I realized this must be how Mom feels most of her days and I felt so sorry for her I wanted to die even more.

Eventually I snuck out of the room and grabbed a beer on my way because outside the real world was waiting. My happy place was the bench in North Boulder Park so I went there. I finished the beer, smoked another cigarette and then threw the pack out because I was never a smoker to begin with. I usually sat on the bench in the early mornings and wasn't expecting to see any of the regulars but the roller-skating woman and the two dads with their daughters showed up. It was a Saturday afternoon, sunny and hot, and the roller skater was wearing light blue shorts instead of her trademark pink tights. The shorts were cut to her hip and flipped up with every stride to expose the white liner underneath. It was sexy as hell, so clearly I was still drunk and feeling the ecstasy.

The dads were drinking coffee even though it was the afternoon. There's a cafe across the street from the park so they probably always met there first; maybe they even traded off days for who bought the drinks and had done it so often the ritual was built into the framework of their lives. It seemed like an easy existence and both men looked at peace with their place in the world. I wanted that tranquility but knew it was out of reach. There was no stillness in my life and things were only getting louder. In the past two days I had mock-raped Alicia, drugged Mel's parents and started drinking again. This was not a recipe for harmony. There's only one path to freedom: truth. I don't know if that's a lyric from a song, a bumper sticker or graffiti I once read in an alley somewhere downtown but in that moment I believed the saying as gospel and got off the bench and walked straight to the police station to turn myself in for drugging the Vanleers.

The walk was less than ten minutes and not nearly long enough to sober up. When I got to the precinct I didn't know what to do so I sat on a long wooden bench and watched the action. None of the cops seemed too busy or like there was anything pressing going on in town. It made me nervous because my crime was probably the worst of the day and would get the most attention and all I really wanted was peace. So I stood up from the bench and picked an older cop with a mustache to give my confession. He had a rugged mountain man look but softness in his eyes suggested he'd hear me out and listen to the whole story about Marty, my nickname and all the reasons why I snapped. I took a deep breath and told myself to act sober and just as I was about to approach the officer Ike and Sara Peterson walked into the station. They held hands and smiled cautiously when they saw me because they wondered what had brought me to such a location.

"Gates my man," Ike said, trying to sound cheerful but not quite pulling it off. "Did someone steal your bike?"

"Ss'at the course," I said in a low, mottled voice. I had spat the words out rather than speaking them.

Sara grabbed my arm. "Oh my God, you're drunk." She sat me down on the bench between her and Ike.

Ike thought the whole thing was hilarious and asked, "So did they pick you up for public intoxication or something?" I shook my head and he said, "Then get out of here before anyone talks to you because as soon as you open your mouth you're busted."

The older cop I was going to confess to approached us and said, "Mr. and Mrs. Peterson? Whenever you're ready." Then he returned to his desk. He was a cantankerous man and there was no chance he would have heard me out.

"Nice guy," Ike said sarcastically.

"Someone broke into Ike's storage unit last night," Sara said. "They took a bunch of his guitars and other memorabilia including some recording session tapes." She shook her head. "That stuff is priceless."

"No way," I said, and swung my head toward Ike. "Who?"

He laughed and replied, "Sober up, bud. We'll put you on the detective squad once you sleep it off." He tousled my hair and stood up, proud of me for being shitcanned, which just goes to show you can take the man out of rock and roll but you can't take rock and roll out of the man. They joined the older cop at his desk and Ike appeared to be taking the whole theft in stride but Sara was distraught. Mothers know best and she probably knew then who the culprit was and that's why she was so upset.

If I confessed to drugging the Vanleers I risked bringing Wade down because the cops would want to know where the drugs came from and even if I didn't rat him out the police would look at the BGC much closer, which put Wade at risk because everyone who worked at the club (and most of the members) knew he was a dealer. Ike and

Sara were two of my favorite people and I didn't want to bring them pain but I couldn't keep another secret.

A policewoman sat on the bench next to me. She was Hispanic, her badge said GARCIA and her pants were extremely tight, which didn't look comfortable because she was at least twenty pounds overweight. "Can I help you?" she asked in an angelic voice. Her skin was almond, her eyes caramel and her teeth brilliantly white. "Are you waiting for someone?" She smiled and I wanted to give her a hug.

"I'm here to tell a secret." I tried to stare into her eyes but couldn't focus.

The pretty policewoman remained unfazed. She grinned like an old friend and suggested, "Why don't you tell me then?"

I smiled back at her and whispered, "My godmother and I had sex. Her name's Alicia Reed. She's a famous psychologist!" I formed my mouth into a big O and covered it with my hand in mock shock.

Garcia considered my story and unclipped a flashlight from her belt and shone it in my eyes. "Let's see . . . you're drunk, you smell like cigarettes and I bet you're not even eighteen." The halo over Garcia's head vanished as quickly as my buzz. She hooked the flashlight back onto her belt without taking her eyes off me and said, "Follow me."

I was seated at a table in an interrogation room and left

alone. Five minutes later Garcia returned with a glass of water and two aspirin. The drink was in a tumbler from a fast-food chain and decorated with an animated character from a Pixar movie as part of a promotional campaign. I wondered if Garcia chose the glass because she thought I was a child and would be comforted by the cartoon. It was a nice gesture but it made me feel worse. She sat down and said, "Talk to me about your godmother, Alicia Reed."

"I made that up," I replied in a very sober voice.

"That's an odd thing to lie about. You could get her in a lot of trouble for saying something like that."

"I didn't think you'd believe me."

"It's not my job to believe you. It's my job to find out if what you say is true or not. So first of all tell me your name, your age and where you live." She didn't have a pad of paper and she wasn't writing anything down which made me relax. I gave her my background info and mentioned I was an athlete and an honor student and had a job at the BGC. I told her I had never been arrested, suspended from school or even put in detention for that matter. I spoke about Mom's mental history, her stay in Arizona and Alicia's role as my guardian. It felt good to talk about it.

Garcia asked, "But if this woman took care of you then why would you make such a horrible allegation about her?"

"I don't know."

She shook her head and replied, "That's not a good enough answer. Where'd you get the booze?"

"I'd rather not say."

She smiled and replied, "I know we're having a nice talk here but you do realize you're still in a police station and I'm still a cop, right?"

"I don't want to get anyone in trouble," I said. I took a sip of water and asked, "Have you ever felt like if one more bad thing happened to you your entire body would shut down and you'd die on the spot?" I paused, then added, "And if it did you'd be okay with it?"

Garcia stared at me with warning in her eyes. She slid her cell phone across the table. "Have an adult come pick you up and I'll let you go."

"Thank you." The screen of her phone showed a picture of a little boy in a Superman costume. "Yours?" I asked, pointing at the image. She nodded proudly and I looked at the little boy again and said, "He looks happy." Then I called Lu.

Lu didn't answer so I left him a message. Twenty minutes later Garcia led him into the room and waited outside the door. The last time I had seen Lu he was wearing windmill pj's. He had since changed into a red and white checkered oxford shirt and blue shorts embroidered all over with red lobsters. Not an upgrade. He stood in the corner and tried to look all hard like he was a real cop.

"Let me guess," I said. "You're with the Kennebunkport Picnic Police."

Lu nodded a sarcastic ha-ha and said, "Here's the deal, the guy in Aspen is coming tomorrow so you can either stay or play."

"That's awfully big of you."

"You think I came down here for fun?"

"No, I thought you did it to be nice."

"Nice? You stole five hundred bucks from me."

"You called my mom a liar."

"She did lie!"

"I know! Why do you think it hurt so much?" Our voices were raised and Garcia could hear us through the door.

Lu took a long breath and said, "Let me explain something to you, okay? They're gonna take my house. I can't pay the mortgage. That's why I've been living in the storage room." He shrugged his shoulders and frowned. "Happy?"

I was the one who had come to the police station to bare my soul but it was Lu who did all the confessing. He looked relieved and I envied him. I wanted to ask what it was like on the other side of the bridge. "Ten G's is a lot of money," I said. "Put it in the bank and get your house back."

"Forty is better than ten and if I want financial advice I'll call Jim Cramer. Are you playing or are you staying?"

"On one condition. You and Wade have to give Ike Peterson his stuff back."

Lu gave me a long look with no indication how he'd reply. For a gambler who was always losing he had a helluva poker face. "Deal," he said, and we left it at that.

Officer Garcia looked at me funny when we left. She had more questions than answers. Having Lu as my chaperone didn't help. Lu and I walked out of the building and stood on the sidewalk. He gazed back at the police station and in his Confucius voice said, "Girl who sit on judge's lap get honorable discharge."

My bike was still at the course so Lu gave me a ride back. When we got to the club Melanie's car was one of the few left in the parking lot. She stood in front of the clubhouse's glass doors etched with the BGC's insignia and talked to Pam, which reminded me my caddy bib was still under the couch in Marty's study. They abruptly stopped talking at my arrival and Pam disappeared through the doors. Mel jogged over to me and said, "Okay, what the hell is going on?"

"You mean your parents?" I smiled like everything was cool. "They're wasted. I had to drive them home."

"Pam said Mom was practically sitting in your lap in the golf cart. What were you guys doing out there?"

"I was sitting in between your mom and your dad, Mel. No one was in anybody's lap. What else did Pam say?"

Mel shut her eyes and shook her head. "You should have seen Mom at the party last night. She was draped over every man she talked to and dirty danced with one of the cops from the mayor's table. I think she's having a midlife crisis slash sexual awakening so if she was all over you on the golf course it wouldn't surprise me."

"That's your dad's job, Mel."

The comment nearly knocked her over, which was my intention, to punish her suspicions so they wouldn't return. Mel and I never spoke about her dad's fondness for me because that's how she wanted it and I loved her so I granted her that wish. "Why would you say that?" Mel asked.

"Because I had to babysit your parents today and now you're coming at me like I did something wrong."

"Did you? You're being awfully defensive. Were you in the den with them?"

"You mean after I was nice enough to drive them home? No. I figured getting them to the front door was a good enough deed for the day."

We could have gone back and forth like that till dark but that wasn't our style so I grabbed Mel's hand and kissed her cheek. "Listen, it's been a long day and all I want to do is take a shower and go to bed so can I sleep over at your house tonight?" I was banking on Mel's parents being passed out so I could sneak down to the den in the middle of the night and grab my caddy bib. I don't know why I lied to Mel about being in the den with her parents. I guess I was trying to keep an already messy situation cleaner, which was dumb because lies always makes things messier.

Mel smiled. "You really want to sleep over?"

"I do."

"Is that all?"

I gave her a playful look and replied, "Of course not."

"Then let's go."

I had struck so many deals that day I could no longer keep track of my tab. When we got to Mel's place her parents were still out cold in the den and we went upstairs undetected. After a long hot shower and two mouthfuls of Listerine my breath was fresh and my hair smelled like Mel's passion fruit conditioner. She waited for me under the sheets and I sat at the foot of the bed and faced away from her.

"Know what hurts my feeling the most?" she asked. "How easy it is for you to control yourself around me."

I looked at her and replied, "How can such an awesome girl be so insecure?"

"Give me something to feel secure about. Make me feel pretty."

"You're so much more than pretty. Don't you get that?"

"Thanks, but tonight all I want is to feel pretty." She smiled and pulled down the sheets.

I lay next to her and as soon as we kissed I knew I wouldn't get a boner until I told her the truth. But the day had been too long and Mel didn't want a heart-to-heart. She wanted me to fumble with her bra, mount her awkwardly and cum much too quickly. She wanted the quintessential experience of two virgins having sex. She wanted what I could never give her.

I pulled her in close and whispered I loved her and then drifted off to sleep as I dreamt about her footprint in the sand.

i only had eyes for mel

*t*he next morning Mrs. Vanleer woke us up. Had she not peered into Melanie's room we might have slept all day. She was wearing a white bikini and had just been swimming. Her hair was wet and her bathing suit clung to her body. Judging by her nipples the water was cold. "Rise and shine," she said, and sauntered out of the room. The bottoms of her bikini were wedged up her crack and her entire right butt cheek was exposed.

"Did she even see me?" I asked.

"How could she not?" Mel replied.

"But she didn't say anything."

Melanie groaned and said, "If she's drunk again I'm running away."

My head pounded, my tongue felt like sandpaper and

the inside of my mouth tasted like a rotten tomato. Then I saw the time. It was eleven in the morning; my match was in an hour. I jumped out of bed and threw on my clothes. They reeked of cigarettes. "I should be at the course right now. Lu's probably freaking out."

Mel was in no rush to get dressed. "So how much're you playing for?" Her voice had an edge. She was pissed I passed out on her and bruised her ego, again.

Mel's room wasn't very girly because she wasn't very girly. Perfume bottles and teddy bears and beads and candles were too frivolous. Her desk and shelves were organized with neatly stacked novels and notebooks. She kept her environment straightforward and orderly, which was how she lived her life and another reason to love her. I didn't want to tell her about the match because the truth would freak her out like every other honest thing about me.

She continued her tirade: "Everyone knows about Lu's matches. Other than Wade being a dealer it's the worst-kept secret at the club. Just like everyone knows my parents were wasted yesterday and that you were flirting in the golf cart with Mom and her new boobs."

"I wasn't flirting with your mom." I threw Mel's shirt on the bed but she didn't reach for it. Time was ticking. I pointed at her shirt and said, "I'm really in a rush."

Melanie pushed the shirt away and stared into space. I

put myself in her line of vision but she turned her head. I headed for the door and when I reached the hallway turned around and said, "I'm playing for forty thousand dollars today so right now your silent treatment seems a little trivial."

Mom called the Vanleers' house a McMansion. The large stucco home was accented with stone trim and had pillars at the front door. A balcony stretched across the entire side of the house facing the foothills. All the properties on the Vanleers' block have large front and back lawns, which is rare in Boulder. The street is one of the most desired locations in town. Mom talked about getting a listing there all the time. Inside, the hallways are wide, the ceilings high and the foyer is bigger than the lobby in Alicia's office building. The floors of the entryway are some kind of fancy wood imported from South America that have to be mopped with an herbal soap and organic oil blend. This was explained to me one day by the Vanleers' housekeeper, Mindy, a single mother of three transplanted from Rhode Island. Mindy was as salty as her native state's coastal air and sneered that the Vanleers spent more money on floor soap than she did on her kids' food. I inspected the French label and colorful logo on the jug of detergent and said, "Yeah but have you ever tasted this stuff? It's amazing." Mindy's never liked me since.

Mrs. Vanleer waited in the foyer. She wore large sunglasses and held a towel in one hand and a beverage in the other. Mindy was off to the side dusting an Oriental vase. We crossed eyes as I came down the stairs and she was pleased to witness the unfolding scandal of my being caught spending the night. Mel chased down the stairs after me and Mrs. Vanleer said, "Both of you, follow me," and headed out the door.

An old Volkswagen Beetle I had never seen before was parked in the driveway. Neither Mel nor her mother acknowledged the car. We passed through a black iron fence and entered a sanctuary of flagstone and flowered landscaping that surrounded a black granite pool. Classical music played from speakers disguised as boulders and umbrellas shaded plush lounge chairs. I could have stayed there all day.

"Why are you taking us to the pool?" Mel asked. "I have to drive Gates to the golf course."

"Too bad," Mrs. Vanleer replied. "You both have some explaining to do."

We filed toward the pool and made a small circle by the deep end. I was expecting Mrs. Vanleer to start lecturing us but Mel spoke first. "What happened yesterday?" she asked.

Mrs. Vanleer tried to place her hand on Mel's shoulder but Melanie stepped away and her mom stumbled before catching her balance. "Honey, your father and I are terribly sorry. We embarrassed you in front of the entire club and we embarrassed ourselves in front of Gates and we have no excuse." The apology would have been much more heartfelt if she hadn't slurred her words and wobbled as she spoke.

"Are you guys getting divorced?" Mel asked her.

Mrs. Vanleer gulped her drink and asked, "Is that what this is about?"

"I'm not sure what this is about," Mel said. "I guess it's about a lot of things, like why you were flirting with my boyfriend yesterday."

I didn't dare speak. Mrs. Vanleer's nipples pressed through her slinky bathing suit because a lone puffy cloud blocked the sun, which gave a slight nip (or two) to the air. Seeing the two women standing next to each other made it easy to understand why Mel felt insecure about her mom now that her mom's skinny frame had large perfectly shaped breasts. Mel caught me staring at Mrs. Vanleer and said, "Gates, tell me the truth. Your clothes reek of cigarettes and so did the den and you can deny it all you want but Pam saw you and Mom in the golf cart and she said you guys were practically on top of each other."

"Who's Pam?" asked Mrs. Vanleer.

"She serves drinks at the club but she wants a job from Marty," I explained.

"Serving him drinks?" Mrs. Vanleer mused. "That'll keep her busy."

"I'm glad this is such a joke to you Mom," Mel said.

"Of course it's a joke! Listen to what you're saying, honey. It's absurd."

"I caught you half naked and passed out drunk in the den at two o'clock in the afternoon and it doesn't get any more absurd than that!" Mel shot back.

The sun finally slipped out from behind the cloud and in the bright light Mrs. Vanleer's white bathing suit became see-through. I couldn't look away from the circular brown shades of her nipples and thin black stripe of her pubic hair. Mel caught me ogling her mother again and shouted, "Take a picture, it'll last longer!" and shoved me in the water.

I blew out the air in my lungs and sank to the bottom of the pool and stayed down there as long as possible. Mrs. Vanleer was lying in a chaise when I came up for air. The classical music from the hidden speakers had switched from violins to piano. Half her drink was gone. "Your ride to the golf course just drove away," she informed me.

"I was afraid of that," I said.

The sunlight continued to work its magic on the white bikini fabric. The implants in Mrs. Vanleer's breasts stood at attention and her legs were spread wide and hung loosely off each side of the chaise. "Were you really staring at me, or is Melanie acting insecure again?" she asked.

I should have lied but I didn't want to throw Mel under

the bus. "I was looking," I admitted. "Your bathing suit's completely see-through," I added as an explanation.

Mrs. Vanleer smiled and replied, "Mother-daughter relationships are tricky but Mel should know nothing would ever happen between you and me. Don't you agree?"

"Obviously," I replied.

"I'm glad we have an understanding."

I wasn't sure if I'd just agreed to something I shouldn't have. Mrs. Vanleer pulled her towel from underneath her body and held it out for me. "Take your clothes off and put them in the dryer. I'll drive you to the course in twenty minutes."

"Take my clothes off?" I asked. She was way too drunk to drive and I worried how I'd get to the course.

"Please," she said, "so you don't leave a trail of water through the house." She took her sunglasses off, reclined her chaise and closed her eyes.

I stepped behind her chair and out of her line of vision and peeled off my wet clothes. They dropped to the flagstone with a loud plop. Mrs. Vanleer shimmied the straps of her bikini top off her shoulders and rolled onto her stomach, which faced her in my direction. Fortunately I'd already wrapped the towel around my waist. She unhooked her top to sun her back and I quickly headed to the house to dry my clothes and reclaim my caddy bib.

The mystery VW Bug was still in the driveway. The

foyer was empty except for a bucket, a mop and the fancy French detergent. I walked to the laundry room and put my clothes in the dryer. The skirt and shirt Mrs. Vanleer had worn the day before were set on top of the dryer washed, ironed and folded. They were as neat as the stacks of notebooks in Melanie's room. Nothing in the house appeared to be out of place except me.

I ran to the den to get my caddy bib but Mindy was there. She dumped the ashtray into a garbage bag and saw me standing in the doorway draped in a towel and continued to work like I wasn't even there. I wandered back to the dryer. The laundry room was in the rear of the Vanleers' house and shared a short hallway with a small guest room. Voices came from the room. The door was propped open with a sneaker to create a draft and left a two-inch crack to see and listen through. Marty was getting a massage from a shirtless young man whose sculpted chest was tan and hairless. A towel was draped over Marty's midsection and he lay facedown on a portable massage table. Spa music played from an iPod speaker port on the floor next to the masseur's oils and his shirt. The masseur smiled and concentrated on his work. Marty moaned and said, "Ugh, I feel like I got run over by a truck."

The masseur chuckled and replied, "Have another late one last night?"

"All I know is I woke up in my den at four A.M. wearing

my golf shoes from the day before." Marty laughed. "I don't even remember coming home from the course." He laughed harder. "And you wanna know the best part? My wife was passed out right next to me!"

The masseur laughed. "You guys are out of control."

Marty groaned and replied, "My head feels like it got stuck in a paint mixer."

The masseur kneaded the soles of Marty's feet and gave him the foot massage he had wanted so badly. Then he stepped away from the table and said, "Flip over." Once Marty was on his back the young man slid his hand beneath the towel and said, "This'll make you feel better."

I backed away from the door and right into Mrs. Vanleer, who'd snuck up behind me. She whispered into my ear and I could smell the booze on her breath, "He's been in there almost an hour. Right now he should be on his back getting what he paid for." She pulled me into the laundry room and shut the door. She was wrapped in a white terry cloth robe and said, "Turn around for a minute."

A framed lithograph of a brightly colored geometrical oval the size of a full-length mirror hung on the wall in front of me. The glass of the frame had been so well cleaned by Mindy it reflected Mrs. Vanleer's image behind me. She threaded her arms out of the robe and placed it on the dryer. I waited for her to look up and notice but she kept her head bowed as she slowly slid one bikini strap off her arm and then the other. With one hand she released the top's clasp between her breasts and draped it on the washing machine. She lifted her head but her eyes were closed as she gingerly stepped out of her bottoms. She turned sideways to grab her shirt off the dryer, which gave me an impressive side view of her new curves. The shirt stopped just above her waist and she turned her backside to me and very slowly she slid her skirt up her legs. Once she was zipped and buttoned she said, "Okay, you can turn around now." She took my place facing the artwork as if we were dancing a routine we'd practiced many times and said, "Your clothes are probably dry by now if you'd like to put them on."

I stood there frozen because I wasn't about to do a strip-tease for Melanie's mom and when she realized I wouldn't play along she looked at me via our reflection in the glass and said, "I can see you! This glass is like a mirror! Why didn't you say something?" She was a shitty actress and her drunkenness didn't help her performance.

"I didn't notice," I said.

She looked at me angrily and replied, "I can't believe you didn't say anything. What kind of a boy are you?" Then she stormed away.

I grabbed my clothes from the dryer and put them on even though they were still wet and left through the front of the house. The microwave in the kitchen read 11:35. I hoped the den would be empty so I could grab my caddy bib but Mindy was still in there. When I got outside Mom was in the Vanleers' driveway and sat on the hood of her car as she listened to her cell phone. She hung up when she saw me and shouted, "So! This is where you've been hiding all night! I've been calling the Vanleers all morning but their phone is disconnected."

"Marty's getting a massage," I explained. "He probably took the phone off the hook."

Just as I said this the handsome young masseur emerged from the front door carrying his fold-up massage table and basket of lotions. His shirt was draped over his shoulder and his muscles flexed with the strain of transporting his gear. He paused in the sun next to us and said, "Days like today make me feel like a pudgy, naked, winged child just shot an arrow through my butt." Then he walked away. Mom and I tried not to look at each other but we couldn't stop ourselves from laughing. The masseur turned around and said, "Took you long enough."

The ice was broken so I spoke first. "Sorry I didn't call to tell you I wasn't coming home last night but I honestly didn't think you'd care."

Mom frowned. "I'm your mother, I'm always going to care."

"Did you even know I was gone until you got home this morning?"

Mom placed her hands atop my shoulders and stood an arm's length away. She looked me right in the eyes and said, "We don't live by the same rules. I'm an adult, you're a child."

"I don't feel like a child."

"Well you still are to me." Mom had a firm grasp on my shoulders and she hung her head. I leaned mine forward so our skulls pressed together. We didn't move or speak. There was a hint of sadness in our silence but it didn't matter because for that moment I was my mother's son and by some flash of luck she had appeared when I needed her.

Mom swatted me on the butt and we broke for her car. "Can you drive me to the golf course?" I asked. "I'm kind of in a rush."

We climbed into the car and Mom took a good look at me. "Are you sure you're up for work? You're white as a ghost."

"I'm just hungry, that's all."

"Why are your clothes all wet?"

"Mel pushed me in the pool."

Mom tsked like she thought that was cute and said, "She likes you . . ."

"Her whole family likes me."

We watched the masseur strap down the ragtop of his Beetle to fit his table in the backseat and Mom asked, "So that's Marty's masseur, huh?" She started the car and threw the transmission into reverse.

Mrs. Vanleer stepped onto the balcony of the master bedroom. She had changed into a black bikini and stared out toward the mountains. Marty appeared behind her and she undid her top as she spun around to face him. He took one look and then walked away. Mrs. Vanleer threw her top at him and turned around to show herself to the world but her house was so closeted and cloaked with landscaping the only person who could see her was me and I only had eyes for Mel.

par for the day

Lu was pacing the parking lot when Mom dropped me off. He threw his hands in the air when he saw us and angrily pointed at his watch. "What's he all bent out of shape about?" Mom asked.

"I'm late," I said. "I'm supposed to tee off in five minutes."

"Oh. I thought you were working today."

"It is work."

Mom gave me a squirrelly look. "I don't even want to know what that means."

"No. You never do."

"Well thank you very little," Mom said, confused by my outburst.

"I'm sorry. I don't even know why I said that."

Mom sat back and sighed. "Why can't we spend even the smallest amount of time together without it turning to shit?"

"I don't know. Today it's not your fault though."

She peered at me with unconvinced eyes. "I know you're mad at me."

"Who said I was mad at you?"

"You do. Every single day."

"How so?" I asked her.

"If I could change the past I would."

"I'm not asking you to." Sometimes I suspected Mom knew about me and Alicia but was too scared to say it. She had talked about "the past" before when referencing her time in Arizona and I often got the feeling that she was waiting for me to apologize for something.

"What about you?" she asked. "Would you change the past if you could?"

"Definitely," I said.

"Then let's let bygones be bygones."

"You say that like I've done something wrong. Did I?"

Mom shook her head but her right eye twitched. We both looked over at Lu. For the special day he was wearing black penny loafers, seersucker shorts, a pink needlepoint belt monogrammed in white and a yellow Ralph Lauren shirt with a jumbo polo player logo covering his entire left breast. To top it off he had bleached his hair blond. I looked at Mom and explained, "He wishes he was someone else."

"I've been there," Mom said. "It's no fun."

"I didn't leave a note about you in Stuart's mailbox," I said.

Mom looked like she'd been slapped. "How do you know about that?"

"There's a lot I know," I replied. "And a lot you don't."

Mom's eyes got watery but she could make herself cry on demand, it was one of her skills as a master manipulator, so I didn't feel badly. "I'm trying to throw you a line here, Gates."

"As I am to you," I quickly retorted. "You wanna be real, then let's be real. Stop talking to me in code and just tell me whatever it is you want to say to me." I suddenly realized how Melanie must feel with me.

"How am I supposed to be real if you're fighting with me?" Mom asked.

"If my being honest feels like a fight to you then we're doomed," I replied.

She snickered and said, "What do you know about being honest . . ." Then she forcefully leaned across me and shoved open the car door.

"How the hell am I supposed to be honest with a fucking freak show?"

"Get out!" Mom yelled. She was shaking and tears were streaming down her cheeks. "Now!!"

"Whatever," I said. "As soon as you act like a mom I'll act like a son."

I hopped out of the car and jogged over to Lu, who waited with his hands on his hips. "Are you trying to give me a heart attack?" He grabbed my shirt. "Why the hell are your clothes wet?" We headed to the storage room. There were a lot of people around including Pam but when we got inside we were alone.

"I'm sorry I'm late," I said. "It's been a crazy morning." I pulled my clubs from the rack and counted them.

Lu buzzed around the room like an angry yellow jacket. "This is the biggest match we've ever had and you can't get here in time to warm up?"

I sat on the bench to put on my spikes. My socks were soggy so I threw them in the trash. "I like your hair," I told him. "Very natural . . ."

Lu stormed into the pro shop and came back a minute later with brand-new socks, shorts, a shirt and he even threw in a belt with the club's logo. He presented them in a tidy stack and said, "Here, I want you to be comfortable out there."

I finished tying my shoes and stood up. "Too late," I said.

Lu extended the pile of clothes toward me again. "It's not a hustle. It's a straight-up match. There's nothing to feel guilty about."

"Don't tell me how to feel," I said, and headed for the tee.

The name of the guy from Aspen was Ed. He looked like a weatherman and had a head of blond hair that suggested he spent more money at the salon than Mindy did on her kids' food. He was somewhere around fifty years old and there was something familiar about his looks but I couldn't place him. Waiting on the tee with him were two other players, Ken and Paula. Ken was in his thirties and slick as a snake's belly. He dressed like Lu but the preppy thing looked good on him. His baseball hat, golf bag and head covers were branded with different crests from famous golf courses on Long Island and he had MEMBER tags for all of them.

Paula was a comedian who'd been in a couple of failed sitcoms. She wasn't really famous and could probably walk 'through an airport without being asked for an autograph but I knew who she was because she played in all the PGA celebrity pro-am events. They always gave her a lot of air-time because she's a very pretty blonde and a better golfer than most of the male amateurs. I'd watched her walk the cliff framed fairways of Pebble Beach when she competed in the AT&T Classic and I'd seen her battle the winds of St. Andrews during the Dunhill Links Championship. When I arrived on the tee in my soggy clothes they must have wondered what they were doing in Boulder Colorado playing with a guy like me.

Introductions were made and we quickly reviewed the

parameters of the match: skins, two grand a hole, with the eighteenth being a jumbo skin worth six thousand dollars. Every man and woman played for themselves and if two players tied the hole the pot carried over, making the next worth four thousand dollars. In the event of another tie the next hole was worth six thousand and so on and so on. Paula would play from the same tees as the guys.

When a foursome convenes on the first tee there's always a keen expectancy that grows until the first shot is struck by each player. Ed led us off and confidently hit one down the middle. Paula went next and outdrove him by fifteen yards. I was predicting great things from Ken what with all his memberships but he swung as jerky and fast as an angry Tourette's patient and his shot never got off the ground and bounced and rolled no farther than a hundred yards from the tee. When his ball came to rest Paula said, "Nice putt, Ken."

Ed was silent while I teed up my ball and I got the feeling he was hoping I'd rip one fifty yards past all of them. Sometimes when someone is rooting for you you can just feel it, which makes sense because you can always tell when the opposite is true. I hadn't swung a club in two days, my clothes were damp and I was starving. The driver felt foreign in my hands and there was no synchronicity between my upper and lower body during my practice swings. I stood still and shut my eyes to envision my shot but all I could see was Mrs. Vanleer's profile in the laundry room.

Lu could tell something was wrong and pulled me to the side of the tee. "What's going on? You look like you're about to puke."

"I don't know. I feel funny."

Paula clapped her hands and said, "Hey, Twilight, you gonna play golf or talk to Shanghai Barbie all day?"

I tugged two balls into the creek that divides the first and eighteenth fairways and was promptly out of the hole. Paula didn't make a peep and her silence was far more damning than a wisecrack. Fortunately she and Ed tied the hole with pars so the pot carried over.

I managed to get my drive in play on the second hole along with everyone else. Ken and I shared a cart. He worked in "Finance" and was visiting Ed to raise money for his hedge fund.

"What's a hedge fund?" I asked him.

"Right now it's something you want to stay as far away from as possible." He laughed and added, "Don't tell Ed that though!" Then he laughed even harder. According to Ken, Ed was a self-made "gazillionaire" who had his fingers in many industries including manufacturing industrial air compressors, bottling plants, fiber optics, Dubai real estate and pharmaceutical nanotechnology.

"So ten grand really isn't that much money to him," I said.

Ken laughed. "He spent that much just flying us here."

"You flew here?"

"The only way Ed travels is in his jet."

We'd arrived at my ball. I had about 170 yards to the hole with a good angle to the pin so all the shot required was a stock eight-iron but my mind was stuck on Ed and the fact that he owned a jet. "Why would he spend ten grand just to play for thirty?" I asked.

Ken shrugged. "It's the only way he knows how to make it interesting."

I shanked my shot into a bush and was out of the hole. Ed watched from across the fairway and tried to hide his disappointment. He went next and fanned his ball right of the green into a patch of reeds. Paula must have made a funny joke because Ed laughed and waved her off to drive to the green alone so he could walk the rest of the hole and enjoy the beautiful day. Ken ended up sinking an eight foot putt to tie Paula with a par and we moved on to number three, which was now worth six G's.

Three is the hardest hole at the BGC: dogleg left, uphill, that measures 460 yards to a tiny green as crooked as the Leaning Tower of Pisa. A huge tree blocks the left side of the fairway so you either have to hit a monster drive to clear it or bail out right, which leaves a tough second shot.

Both Paula's and Ken's drives got eaten by the tree but Ed cleared it with a bomb straight down the middle. He bowed when Paula and Ken applauded and grandly motioned for me to go next.

I was shaking. It was all too much: Mel's justified and growing impatience with me, Mrs. Vanleer's drunken striptease in the laundry room, Marty's masseur, my fight with Mom, Lu's insane hair and outfit, and to cap it all off a forty-thousand-dollar golf match with three misfits who'd arrived by private jet. Golf had been my sanctuary and even that was gone.

Paula said to me, "Hey, Oliver Twist, you gonna hit or what?"

I hooked my drive out of bounds and Ed won the hole easily. I continued to play like a dog but fortunately the three of them tied the next six holes. When we made the turn from the front nine to the back nine I ran into the clubhouse to use the bathroom. Caddies weren't allowed in there but I was a guest that day and no one looked at me twice. Except for Pam who rushed over from behind the bar and blocked the door to the men's room. "What do you want Pam? I gotta piss."

"I want to know what you did to the Vanleers yesterday."

"I saved their drunk asses is what I did."

"Melanie said she found her mom half naked in her den and she's pretty sure you were there with her."

I tried to step around her but she shadowed me.

"We all know it wasn't Marty taking off her clothes," Pam said.

"Bye Pam," I said, and pushed past her into the bathroom.

When I emerged Lu was waiting with a Gatorade and a hot dog. We sat at an empty table and Lu watched me eat. He waited until I was finished and then said, "Talk to me."

"What?"

"Are you fucking up on purpose or are you just fucking up?"

"I'm not doing it on purpose but what you did was pretty lame."

"I needed your help."

"And I needed yours."

"So," Lu shrugged. "We helped each other."

"It doesn't feel that way to me."

Lu scanned the faces in the clubhouse. People ate lunch and soaked in the view of the golf course. He inhaled with satisfaction and said, "There isn't a single person in this room who hasn't been faced with a crisis and if you asked each and every one of them how they managed they'd all say they did the very best they could."

It was hard to take Lu seriously as a blond. I expected him to use his Confucius voice and say something like *Crowded elevator smell different to midget*, but he was trying so I told him, "If it was the best you could do it was the best you could do," and forgiving him made me feel better.

We reconvened on the tenth tee. The hole was now worth fourteen thousand dollars. I was the last to arrive and when Ed saw me he said, "Alright, Boy Wonder, time for you to step it up. I could've stayed in Aspen if all I was gonna do was play against these two nitwits."

I grabbed my driver from my bag and the club felt familiar again. I made a few loose practice swings and my arms, hips and shoulders were finally in synch. When it was my turn to tee off I said to the group, "I never played a hole worth fourteen thousand dollars before but I think I'm gonna like it." Then I ripped one past all of them.

I ended up with an easy birdie putt to win the pot but intentionally missed because a tie made the next hole worth sixteen thousand dollars and I'd never played one of those either.

Eleven is a six-hundred-yard par 5 with water down the left and trees down the right but if you miss far enough right you can land it in the thirteenth fairway and have a good angle for the second shot so that's where I hit my drive just for the hell of it. Something told me if we kept tying holes the day would only get more entertaining and I never thought I'd play for forty thousand dollars again so why not enjoy the ride?

Ed's spirits had come alive and he gave every shot a

nickname. When I pushed my drive way right he called it a "Rush Limbaugh," and when his ball landed in the water and miraculously squirted back onto the fairway he called it a "Teddy Kennedy." Ken played the hole beautifully and all he had to do was sink a three-foot putt to win the sixteen grand but he choked and everyone erupted with cheers because the cash was safe.

We had to gather ourselves on the number-twelve tee. Eighteen grand was on the line and the four of us stood staring at the pin tucked 230 yards away in the back top shelf of the green. Paula teed up her shot and looked out at the difficult hole. She took a few breaths and said, "Man, this is a real dickfore."

"What's a dickfore?" Ken asked.

Paula said, "Figures . . . ," then put a great swing on her ball and landed it on the green.

The game was officially on and we tied the next five holes. By the time we reached seventeen the hole was worth twenty-eight thousand. Lu was pale and the starch in his collar was limp. Twice I caught him sipping from a bottle of Pepto. The pink syrup was the perfect accessory for his preppy attire. Everyone's skills started to crack with only two holes left and so much money at stake. We all got our drives in the fairway but then Ken topped his second shot, Ed hit his in the bunker and Paula reached the green but was forty feet from the pin. That left the door open for me to hit it tight but I choked and flared one high and right that landed almost as far away from the hole as Paula's shot. I never even hit my putt though because Ed holed his bunker shot and then Paula drained her forty-footer right on top of him. The whole scene was completely surreal, which was pretty much par for the day.

Eighteen was worth thirty-four thousand dollars. Ed smiled serenely as he stood on the tee and looked down the fairway into some part of his life that no one else understood. After a moment of introspection he said, "This here's what I call a Paris Hilton: one expensive hole."

Ed and Paula both hit beauties down the middle. Ken was trying to keep his composure but somewhere deep inside knew his elite course memberships couldn't swing the club for him and gambling with other people's money in a hedge fund felt a whole lot different than playing for your own on a golf course. He barely got the ball in play and was no longer a factor. I teed off with a hybrid so I'd be short of Ed and Paula. This would let me hit into the green first and hopefully knock it stiff to make them choke.

Ken drove us to our balls and I was nervous and full of adrenaline but instinct kicked in and all the years of practice and repetition summoned a trace of muscle memory to swing the club for me and my ball landed in the middle of the green and got a lucky bounce toward the pin. Ed went next and nuked his shot way over the green. He stared at his club in confusion at how far the ball flew, but it seemed like an act. That left it up to Paula. She'd played all over the world, with celebrities and professional golfers, under the glare of TV crews and the public's perception of her as a failed comic actress. She was living that strange curse of being famous and nobody at the same time. We all live dual lives—who we know we truly are versus how the rest of the world perceives us. Perhaps this is what she was thinking about when she took her shot. Something other than golf was on her mind because she chunked it big-time and the ball flew only twenty feet.

The rest of the match was academic. I won with a par, but a bogey would've gotten the job done. Paula, Ken and I waited in the parking lot while Ed and Lu settled up in Lu's office. Pam's shift had ended and when she walked past us on her way toward her car she gave me a dirty look. Paula noticed and commented, "Damn, Gates, what'd ya do to her? Give her an STD?"

"She wishes," I replied before realizing how retarded it would sound.

Paula looked me up and down and sarcastically said, "Yeah, I bet."

"Did you chunk your second shot on eighteen on purpose?" I asked her.

"Why would I do that?"

"That's what I'm trying to figure out. I'm also a little

suspicious about Ed's shot over the eighteenth green. A miss that bad can only be intentional. Trust me, I know."

She grinned and said, "You got a nice short game. Hang on to that putter even if it lets you down."

Ed and Lu were walking up the steps toward us. They laughed and patted each other on the back. We said our goodbyes and Lu and I watched them drive away in an unassuming rental car back to Ed's private jet.

"Did Ed tell you how he found out about me?" I asked Lu.

"Your friends from Omaha."

"They knew they got hustled?"

"Everybody figures it out eventually. You live and you learn." He shook my hand and said, "You working tomorrow?"

I laughed and said, "Uh, I think you owe me thirty-four hundred dollars, Lu."

"That was before you got arrested. Once I bailed you out the deal changed."

"You promised me ten percent."

Like Confucius Lu said, "Promises like baby, easy to make but hard to keep."

I could have made a stink but I knew Lu would be back and for some reason I suspected Ed would want more action too; I just couldn't figure out his motivations.

candlelit epiphanies

i went to Lucky's and sat in a booth because I often did some of my best thinking there. My fight with Mom that morning made me suspect she knew about Alicia and wanted to talk. That's why she showed up at the Vanleers'. She was trying to be nice to break the ice but things fell apart so quickly we never really got talking, which was what always happened. It was just as much my fault as it was hers. We were great at avoiding the real conflict by creating superficial ones instead.

After I ordered I called Timmy Timmy Timmy to apologize for my drunk dialing the day before but he didn't answer his phone. He might have been busy but knowing Timmy Timmy Timmy he was still too mad to deal with me. I really didn't blame him.

The roller-skating woman from the park walked into Lucky's and at first I didn't recognize her because she was dressed in blue jeans and a white button-down shirt. Her hair was gathered into a ponytail as long as an actual pony's tail and she was smaller out of her skates and looked a lot less crazy without the headphones and pink tights. She walked with an elegant stride and humble demeanor and looked out at the world through pale blue eyes set in deep, wise wrinkles. Clutched in her arm was an encyclopedia bookmarked in the middle. I couldn't take my eyes off her and when she spotted me she approached my table and said, "Thanks for the wind chime. Mind if I join you?" She sat down and took a long look at me.

"So I guess you're wondering why I hung a wind chime on your porch," I said.

"It doesn't happen every day." She cracked a soothing smile.

"Do you like it?"

"It's fabulous. The wind has no color so you've given it a voice. Everything should have a voice, no?"

Her bookmark was a folded sheet of music. "Do you play an instrument?" I asked her.

"The cello."

"Are you good?"

Her eyes fell to the table like I'd embarrassed her but when she looked up her face was filled with confidence.

"I'll tell you what, when we're done eating let's sit on my porch and I'll play for a while and let you be the judge."

"You want to play me the cello?"

"Bach's six suites to be exact."

"I thought Bach played the piano."

She grinned and said, "That's probably Mozart you're thinking of. Bach played a lot of instruments. He was an extremely talented organist but his real gift was composing. He lost both his parents when he was fourteen." She looked at me as if she expected the last bit of trivia to have a special meaning.

"Why do you say it like that?" I asked her.

"You look like a sweet boy. It always makes me sad to see you sitting alone so early in the morning."

"I had no idea I looked so pathetic," I said.

She laughed gracefully. "We'll fix you up in no time after dinner okay?"

I accepted the offer and as we ate she told me about her life as a concert cellist. She'd performed in seventy-four countries on six continents for audiences big and small, from royalty to the homeless in Central Park. I told her my golf clubs were my instruments and how I had played in a match that day for forty thousand dollars. She thought I was joking and even I began to crack up at my story about Ed, Paula and Ken. The laughter alone was worth the price of a million wind chimes.

When dinner was over we walked back to her house and I sat on the railing of her porch while she went inside to get her cello. She set up a chair six feet away from a chaise longue and told me to lie back and close my eyes. It was a warm night with a warm breeze and to make the evening even more hypnotic she lit candles in hurricane vases that illuminated the porch in a steady yet unpredictable incandescence. She began to tune her instrument and said, "People have all kinds of reactions when they listen to the suites. They were written to explore every emotion, so explore." A slight breeze jostled the chimes and she began to play.

For reasons I didn't understand the music brought me back to the Halloween night when Alicia and I lived in Aspen. I was dressed up like a doctor and Alicia wore a nurse's costume. She turned off all the lights in the house to avoid trick-or-treaters and we ate a candlelit dinner in the kitchen with the shades drawn. She cooked black and orange pasta and served pumpkin beer. That night was the first time we allowed ourselves to have fun since Mom had tried to kill herself and even though she was still in a hospital in Arizona it felt okay to celebrate something as goofy as Halloween.

Alicia hadn't yet laid a finger on me but had crossed every boundary that should stand between a forty-year-old woman and the fifteen-year-old godson in her trust. She would call me into her room to ask me about the weather when she was deciding what to wear and always waited for my report in sexy lingerie. She'd come into the bathroom while I was taking a shower to discuss the menu for dinner. She had a Jacuzzi below my bedroom window and after she'd send me to bed she'd get in the hot tub naked with a glass of wine and sit on the edge of the whirlpool completely exposed. Masturbating to Alicia's hot tub show became as nightly a ritual as brushing my teeth. And then there was her nurse's costume on Halloween: white patent leather heels, white thigh-high stockings, a short white skirt, a red satin bra worn under a tight white shirt, red lipstick, black librarian glasses and her hair pinned up beneath a paper tiara with a red cross.

We stayed up late, drank the holiday beer and danced to the radio. Alicia stuck her arms out like a mummy when they played "The Monster Mash." She twirled and spun and lip-synched the words, which made me laugh. The next song was a ballad and we slow-danced. I got a boner and she pretended not to notice. Her hands were clasped around the small of my back and mine rested on the ridge of her butt. At some point I could no longer hear the radio, could no longer feel my legs or see any of the room around us. I looked at Alicia's face and she looked back and then I leaned in to kiss her. She kept her mouth closed but didn't pull away and I rubbed her ass with one hand and her breasts with the other and she just stood there with her hands locked together on the small of my back while I explored the topography of her body and tried to get her to open her mouth and give me her tongue. But she wouldn't. Imagine going over Niagara Falls in a barrel. The most exhilarating and terrifying moment would be those final few seconds where the massive drop-off appears and there's no turning back. That is how I remember leaning in to kiss Alicia.

■

The cello paused and when the second suite began I thought about the morning after Halloween. When I woke up the house was empty and Alicia didn't leave a note saying where she'd gone or when she'd be back and I sat around dreading the awkward moment of her return. After a while I began to snoop. I examined her medicine cabinet, stared at the clothes hanging in her closet and fingered through her underwear. Her nurse's costume was piled on a chair in the corner of the room. Just seeing it made me horny and I wondered what was wrong with me. I didn't want to want her but I'd had an erection from the moment I stepped into her room and before I could stop myself I undressed at her bedside, climbed on top of her sheets and started to masturbate with a pair of her panties.

That's when Alicia arrived home and caught me. Her

entrance was so silent, her timing so precise, I had a hunch even then she'd been spying on me.

■

The cello halted on a low note that echoed eventually to silence. Everything went perfectly still until a warm gust of wind clanged the chimes at the exact moment when the third suite began. My memory returned to the look on Alicia's face when she found me playing my instrument on her bed. Her eyes filled with horror but she didn't run from the room or step into the hallway to let me get dressed. Instead she sat next to me and said, "This has to stop right now. What you did to me last night was wrong. And now this? I feel very awkward knowing you're sexualizing our relationship."

My pants were tangled around my ankles and I was too embarrassed to move so I sat there and spread her panties over my crotch to cover myself. My boner wasn't going anywhere and Alicia's tan silk underwear looked like a teepee on my lap. Alicia's eyes passed over my waist and she kept talking, "It's my fault. I guess I just thought you'd never go there. I mean your mother is in a mental institution right now. How could you even be thinking of sex? And with me? That's really sick. Seriously. I should take you to a doctor."

"I don't want to go to a doctor."

"You might have to. There's something seriously wrong with you."

"I'm sorry. It won't happen again."

"It better not. If it does we'll have to lock you up in the same hospital as your mom." She shook her head in disbelief and in an angry tone asked, "Do you know what she'd do if she found out about this? She'd try to kill herself again and it would be your fault."

■

I started to cry really hard, in Aspen and on the roller skater's porch as well. The melody of the cello mixed with the memory moved me to a deeper understanding of Alicia's manipulations than I had ever possessed before and my tears were filled with forgiveness for myself as the third suite ended.

When the fourth suite began I stayed with the recollection of crying on Alicia's bed as I tried to hide my boner beneath her panties. I reached forward to pull up my pants and Alicia's underwear slid to the mattress. My trousers were twisted and knotted at my feet and I panicked as I struggled and failed to pull them up. Alicia softly placed her underwear back on my boner to cover me and said, "Hey, there's nothing to be embarrassed about. Our bodies are our bodies." But I was in a full-blown red-faced gasping for air between howls of anguish bawl session and nothing was going to sedate me. I felt shame for my lust, confusion for thinking Alicia wanted it, guilt for acting on it and embarrassment for getting caught. And to make matters worse my boner wouldn't go away, which made me even more convinced something really was wrong with me because this was the single greatest moment of distress in my life and I could still maintain an erection.

Alicia was shocked by the intensity of my sobbing. She patted my back and begged me to calm down. She said it was no big deal, it would be our little secret, but her words made me cry harder. Then she stood up and slowly shimmied off her pants and her underwear, which shut me up quick. She sat beside me on the bed and calmly said, "Let me show you something," as she took my hand and put it between her legs. She pinched my fingers against a small string sticking out of her and slowly pulled our hands away until her tampon slid out. She dangled the blood-clotted tampon in front of us and said, "Not that sexy is it?" But her hand had touched my penis when she covered me with her underwear and my fingers had grazed her crotch when she guided them to her tampon and it was all too much and I came with such force the explosion popped her panties into the air. Alicia laughed and exclaimed, "Oh my God I've created a monster!"

■

Alicia knew what she was doing all along. She even admitted it then when she said, *"I've created a monster."* At fifteen I was too young to catch this but the preciseness of the roller skater's bow passing over the cello's strings brought order and clarity to the moment that until then had been obscured with distress. Life is wacky about where and when it gives epiphanies. I'm only seventeen so I haven't had that many but they've all come when I least expected them. Maybe it's their surprise that makes them so meaningful but I think it's their meaningfulness that makes them so surprising. Like when I realized how much I loved Mel that day on the golf course, I just knew I was going to change my life for her. And when I was on the porch listening to the cello I realized that what had happened with Alicia was never my fault.

The wind tousled the chimes when the fourth suite ended as if nature and performer were playing in concert. When the fifth suite started my memory returned to the scene on Alicia's bed in Aspen. After I shot my wad like a violent volcano Alicia walked across her room bottomless and threw away her tampon, then put on the panties I'd been masturbating with, which were splattered with my cum. She went downstairs and I finally managed to get my pants up around my waist and scampered to my room and looked up Mom's "hospital" online. I called the main number but they wouldn't tell me if they had any patients staying there with Mom's name so I called our home in Boulder and the phone had been disconnected. I wanted to ask Mom if I could go to boarding school instead of staying with Alicia but it was like she had vanished off the face of the earth. So I decided to run away, back to home, and see if our house was even still there or if a new normal family had moved in and taken our place. I stayed in my room until dark, then climbed out my window to the roof. Snow was falling and the shingles were frozen and slick. It was a big leap to the yard but I was running for my life so I closed my eyes and jumped.

The cops picked me up on the shoulder of eastbound I-70 by the Glenwood Springs exit forty-five miles away. Two hours later Alicia arrived at the station. Under normal conditions it only takes an hour to drive from Aspen to Glenwood Springs but it was snowing so hard it took her twice as long. She thanked the police and pretended to be mystified by my bizarre behavior but as soon as we were in the parking lot she grabbed my arm and dragged me through the snow. Back then she was half a foot taller and thirty pounds heavier than me. She threw me into the front seat and smacked the hood as she raced around to her side of the car. Then she slammed her door and yelled, "What the fuck am I supposed to do with you!"

Very meekly I replied, "I think I should go to boarding school."

"Not an option."

"I don't want to be a monster."

The music stopped and I'd been too deep in memory to notice the suite was winding down. The final melody of the sixth suite promptly commenced and I smiled with the knowledge I had done my best to not sleep with Alicia. Not even a storm stopped me from running and had I been older with resources I might have made it all the way to Boulder and possibly even to boarding school. But instead I ended up in a roadside motel with Alicia. The storm had forced everyone off the road and we were lucky to get the last room. We climbed into the single king-sized bed at the same time and Alicia turned off the lights. The events of the past twenty-four hours had me upside down and I could no longer distinguish among what I was feeling, what I thought I was supposed to be feeling and what was actually happening. Alicia pushed my boxers down my legs and quickly straddled my waist. I wasn't even aroused. She said, "If this is the only way to keep you in line I'll do it but if your mother finds out she really will kill herself and it'll all be your fault. Do you really want to take that risk?"

"No," I said, but my dick had gotten hard and the tip of my penis was pressed against the warm, wet lips of her vagina and I had never felt what that was like before and her tits were in my face and my dick got even harder and she either lowered herself onto me or I raised my hips into her but either way I only lasted two seconds inside her before I came.

Alicia stared at me intensely as she felt me ejaculate. She lowered her hips and flexed her vaginal muscles so they pulsated around me and with a stern and passionless voice she said, "Too late."

■

The cello mixed seamlessly with the wind chimes as the roller skater manipulated her instrument with instinct and passion. When the music stopped I opened my eyes. The candles in the hurricane vases had burned down to tiny puddles. Tears streamed down the cellist's face and with a smile she swept her arm toward her porch stairs and the world beyond and sent me on my way.

■

The night was young and Mexican was having a party because his parents were in Patagonia on some adult learning vacation. Mexican's mom and dad both came from insanely rich families in Ohio. His dad's family business made some kind of special screw used to build every kind of car dashboard. His mom's family business did something as equally banal and profitable. So they didn't work and instead traveled a lot but their trips always had a charitable slant like visiting some little island halfway around the world to build huts for the villagers. I thought it was pretty cool but Mom called them Trustafarians and said they suffered from Rich Guilt Syndrome. She said if Mexican's parents were so hell-bent on fixing the world they should start in their backyard and they were total hypocrites because if they cared about saving the environment they wouldn't be flying all over the place. But Mom and Mexican's parents had history because after Mom tried to kill herself and went to Arizona they offered to let me live with them rather than drop out of school and move to Aspen. But Mom sent me with Alicia anyway so maybe Mexican's folks remind her of that terrible decision.

All our friends liked Mexican's parents, so when he had a party we kept it quiet and no one smoked inside. I usually avoided parties but I'd always go to Mexican's because the crowd would be small and mellow. It was weird going out without my wingman 3T's and I wasn't sure who I'd hang with. When Timmy Timmy Timmy and I went to parties we'd find a corner and play cards. 3T's always carried a deck and could shuffle like a Vegas dealer and do card tricks. I guess models spend most of their time sitting around waiting to be photographed so they learn how to do that kind of stuff. 3T's and I would hang in the corner because we were shy and insecure but people thought we were cool because we didn't care about socializing. Some of the smartest kids in high school are retarded as soon as you take the textbooks out of their hands.

When I got to the party Mexican, Tap Water, Frostbite and Wade were playing beer pong on the porch. Mexican's pad was on the crest of Mapleton Hill and his parents built a roof deck with some special kind of eco-wood that Mom said was a rip-off and not even environmentally friendly. Attached to the deck was a glass-walled studio where Mexican's dad "worked." He was supposedly an author but one time I tried to buy his books and they were both out of print. Everyone wanted to know what happened the day before with the Vanleers. The rumors around the club ranged from Marty being driven away in an ambulance to Mrs. Vanleer throwing up on the fourteenth tee. I downplayed everything and Wade didn't mention the ketamine so the guys were disappointed. Frostbite said, "Marty's old lady looks halfway decent with the new headlights, eh?"

Everyone nodded and Tap Water said, "Maybe you should *meditate* on those, eh, Fun Buns?"

I shot Frostbite an angry look. He shrugged.

Tap Water wasn't finished. "I gotta hand it to you though, Fun Buns, because there's probably a few dudes out there who've hooked up with both the mother and the daughter, but I bet you're the only one who got the father too!" Tap Water lobbed the Ping-Pong ball into Wade's cup, pointed at him and said, "Drink, Hair . . . I mean, Wade."

I went to get a beer and saw Mel through a window sitting at the kitchen table so I debated whether I should even go inside. Mel was playing quarters with the clique of girls who pretty much ran our high school. When it was Mel's turn she sank five shots in a row and every time chose Mandee Frank to drink. Mandee was the queen of our class and abused her power of popularity by constantly starting infighting among their friends. All the girls were afraid of Mandee except for Mel, and I loved her for that.

Mel busted me watching her through the window and ran outside. She handed me a deck of cards from her pocket. "I brought you these. Thought you might be tempted to drink since Timmy Timmy Timmy's not here and we all know that's a bad idea."

"Why do you do things that like?" I asked.

"Things like what?"

"Things that make me love you."

"I'm just saying you're a bad drunk, Gates. It's not exactly a Hallmark moment."

"I thought you were mad. You pushed me in the pool."

"I don't want to be mad tonight. Tonight I want to be like them." She pointed to the girls in the kitchen. Chatter and laughter blended with the music playing from the stereo in a perfect symphony of youth and rock and roll. "So . . . you in?"

"I can't."

"Can't ever? Or can't right now?"

"Can't right now." I pointed inside and said, "Go make Mandee Frank drink so much she pukes all over herself."

Mel grinned slyly and said, "I'm workin' on it."

"That's why I love you so much."

"I hope you have a better reason than that."

"Got a million of 'em."

"You're really gonna leave me all alone at this party? What if I meet the man of my dreams tonight?"

"He won't be here," I said.

"No? Where will he be?"

"He'll be one good night's sleep and two hard conversations away."

Mel thought this over and said, "Get a good night's sleep, Gates." She kissed me softly on the lips goodbye.

"I'm sorry it's taking me so long." I was talking about fixing myself but she thought I meant about us not having sex. In some ways they were one in the same.

"I'm sure there's a good reason but that's kinda what scares me." She delivered the line like a joke but it was obvious she was being serious. And that was the biggest reason to love her. The girl knew how to be nothing but real.

liars don't know how to love

*I*t was only eight o'clock when I left the party but it felt like midnight. Exhaustion's steady hum vibrated through my bones and it was a good honest tired free of guilt and shame. I looked forward to putting my head on the pillow and enjoying my first good night's sleep in four years. Back home our street was quiet. Mom's car was parked in Stuart's driveway and not hidden in his garage like normal and Stuart's shades were down, which was odd because he usually left them up. Alicia's car was in our driveway so I snuck in through the back door. Thankfully the house was empty and I went straight to bed and slept for twelve hours.

In the morning I felt like a new person and hoped the sensation would stick. Alicia's and Mom's rooms were empty and their beds were still made. The newspaper was at the foot of the driveway and when I walked out to get it a CD in a clear plastic case was on our front step. *THIS IS ME* was written in pink on the disk. It was a recording of the roller skater playing the six suites on her cello. I played it through all the house speakers and leisurely read the front page. The classical music radiated a peaceful cheer into each room and brightened the house like a fresh coat of paint.

Eventually Alicia came home. She was barefoot and wore a plain white sundress with nothing underneath. She stopped just inside the door and smiled and cocked her head. "Ah, Bach. Did you put this on?"

"Yup." I looked back to the paper.

Alicia wanted me to acknowledge she'd been out all night and ask where she'd been but I wasn't about to give her the satisfaction. I didn't hear a car drop her off, which meant she'd walked home, and wherever she'd spent the night was probably nearby since she wasn't wearing shoes. The obvious answer was Stuart's house. It was also the most frightening.

She sat across from me and smiled. Her sundress was so diaphanous (SAT word) that the aureolas (not an SAT word) of her nipples were traceable. "A policewoman stopped by my office yesterday asking questions about you. She said she was concerned because you showed up at the station drunk but I think her visit was to check me out. Did you say anything about us to an Officer Garcia?"

"You mean like we fuck? Yeah but she didn't believe me so you're off the hook."

"Hey you wanted it so don't turn around now and say I molested you. It wasn't like that."

"I was fifteen years old and you had sex with me. It doesn't matter if I wanted it or not."

"If it was so wrong why'd you start it?"

"You started it by walking around the house naked all the time and if you come near me again I'll go back to the police. I'm tired of lying to Mom and besides, I think she might be on to us and for some reason blames me."

"It's been a rough two years for all of us, hasn't it?" she asked sympathetically. We looked in each other's eyes and our bond was still there. We had been each other's co-dependents for so long we seemed destined to take this sick alliance to the grave. Alicia inhaled a sharp breath and said, "There's something you should know. When we lived in Aspen your mom wasn't in Arizona at a mental hospital. She was here in Boulder shacking up with your dad while he remodeled this house for her. She never even went to a hospital. Your dad sent her to a fancy spa for twenty-eight days when he found out she tried to kill herself."

"My dad?"

"He'd been living in the Middle East and showed up

out of nowhere and that's what made your mom supposedly melt down. But I think she was faking because she
wanted his attention and she got a month at Canyon
Ranch and a remodeled home out of the deal."

"My father?"

"He didn't know you existed and she didn't want him
to know so she hid you in Aspen with me. Then he left her
just like I told her he would."

"Who is he? Where's he now?"

"We don't talk about him. I think he moved to Califor-
nia or Cambridge, I can't remember. The guy's a loose
cannon. He was always chasing the next big thing. Sometimes he'd hit it but he usually missed and right now wherever he is he's probably down to his last dollar."

"Was he a golfer?"

Alicia shrugged and dismissively replied, "I don't know,
maybe," because she thought my question was irrelevant.
"Did you really try to have me arrested?"

"I was drunk and you know how pissed I am that you
started doing it again."

"Pissed? I thought it was mutual."

"It was never mutual."

Alicia chuckled and laced her fingers in front of her
chest. She leaned forward like a professor or a priest and
explained, "Gates, if you have an erection and you undress
me and you run your hands along my body and kiss me

with an open mouth and tongue for long periods of time I'm going to have to assume your desire for sex is mutual."

I mimicked her body language, interlaced fingers and all, and replied, "That's like striking a match in a dry field and then blaming the field for catching on fire."

"I see. So you're a victim in all of this."

"You're a famous psychologist. Do I really need to spell it out?"

"I didn't tell you to kiss me, Gates."

"No, but you didn't tell me not to either," I replied.

"Actually I did, several times."

"You knew what you were doing."

She stared me over and said, "You look like hell. Go sit in your mom's steam shower. It'll flush all those toxins out of your system."

Alicia headed to her room and I was happy she didn't try to seduce me. Officer Garcia's visit had spooked her. I didn't know what to make of her story about my father or Mom never being in the hospital. Alicia always said Mom was on the verge of another nervous breakdown to keep me silent so it was puzzling to hear this new version of history. If my father was in Boulder when we were in Aspen, and was in fact a golfer, at least it explained how a custom-made Scotty Cameron putter ended up in our basement. The only thing I knew for sure was that Alicia was trying to manipulate me, but I didn't know to what end.

A steam sounded good especially knowing I was safe from her advances. And that's why I'm an idiot because just as I was beginning to relax and break a nice sweat Alicia came in and rinsed herself off and then lay perpendicular to me so our feet touched.

I sat up and said, "Really?"

She acted confused. "What?"

I immediately stepped out of the shower and standing in the doorway of the bathroom staring directly at my naked dripping wet body were Mom and Melanie. Mom was wearing a wrinkled suit from the day before and Mel was holding my caddy bib.

"Whoa!" I quickly grabbed a towel. "What are you guys doing here?"

"This is *my* bathroom," Mom said.

Mel dangled the caddy bib with two fingers and said, "Look what Mindy found in our den."

"Can you guys give me a second so I can dry off?" I wanted them out of the bathroom so I could warn Alicia not to come out.

"I want an explanation now," Mel said.

"What are you doing in my shower?" Mom asked.

The door to the spa popped open with a thick cloud of steam and Alicia stepped out nude and dripping wet.

Mel dropped the caddy bib and ran. I caught up to her on the street as she got in her car. Mel was a fast runner and it was hard to be swift with a towel tied around my waist.

"Will ya just wait a second?" I pleaded.

"How did your caddy bib get in the den?"

"Come inside and let me put some clothes on. I'll tell you everything."

"And why was your godmother in the steam bath with you? Naked?"

"I'll explain that too."

"No you won't," Mel said. "You'll just lie because all you do is lie."

"None of this is how it looks, I swear."

"It looks like you're hooking up with your godmother and decided to have your way with my mom too."

"I didn't touch your mother."

"Why should I believe anything that comes out of your mouth?"

"Because I love you, Mel."

"Liars don't know how to love." She started her car and drove away.

The cello suites played loudly from the speakers inside. I wanted to turn off all the lights and spark up some candles but the morning was too chaotic for epiphanies. Mom and Alicia shouted at each other in the bathroom and I listened through the door. Alicia said, "You can't have it both ways so you're gonna have to make up your mind!"

Mom yelled back, "Why do you do this to me!"

Alicia screamed, "You're hardly the victim here! You never have been either!"

I pounded the door and shouted, "Let me in!" Then it got real quiet. I knocked again and said, "Open the door Mom. We gotta talk."

There was movement in the bathroom, then Mom replied, "Leave us alone. We're in the middle of something."

"I wanna talk about this now!" I shouted back.

Mom opened the door an inch and said, "Tough nuggets! Now get out of my room."

I stuck my face right up to the small opening and asked, "Who remodeled this house? It couldn't have been Alicia because the whole time we were in Aspen I never saw her with a blueprint or heard her have a conversation with a contractor. So who did it? And how did it get done if we were in Aspen and you were in Arizona? Or were you here all along?"

Mom glared over her shoulder at Alicia then shot me the same nasty scowl. "How dare you!"

"Were you even sick or not? Who's my father? Why doesn't he know about me?"

"He died before you were born!"

"Then tell me this Mom: how does a dead man leave a putter in the basement?"

Mom broke into tears. "Haven't you made me suffer enough?" She slid to her knees and locked the door. She

quickly stopped crying and I tried to hear how Alicia con-
soled her but the bathroom was silent and not even the
steam bath hissed.

The doorbell rang faintly over the cello suites and filled
me with hope Mel had returned but when I opened the
door, still wearing nothing but a towel, Wade and Lu were
there to greet me. Lu wore white slacks and a ship captain's
jacket with gold stripes on the cuffs, epaulets on the shoulders and an anchor crest on the breast pocket. Wade's face
was hidden beneath his visor. I pinched the bridge of my
nose and squeezed my eyes shut and took a moment to
gather myself. With a pleading expression of desperation
on my face I said to them, "Can you guys please take your
sideshow somewhere else today?"

Wade said, "Sorry, Fun Buns. This is serious."

"That's impossible if you guys are involved." I pointed
at Lu and added, "He's dressed for a cruise," to prove my
point.

Wade leaned into the doorway and cocked his head to
listen. "Is that Bach?" He looked at me with a new appreci-
ation and said, "Bach rocks," which proved Ike and Sarah
were doing their best with what they had to work with. My
house must have seemed like a sanctuary with classical
music stirring softness through the air. It's a good thing so
much of life is based on appearances because if everyone's
truths were on display even Maui would feel like Detroit.

Lu stepped in front of Wade and said, "Ed called. He wants to play you for fifty grand on Saturday in Aspen."

"Awesome. Did you tell him you have no money?"

"He's sending his jet tomorrow so you can play a practice round on his course."

"Find someone else."

"He only wants to play you."

"I'll lose on purpose, Lu. You already screwed me out of my last cut, which was three and a half grand, so you can go fuck yourself." I looked at Wade and asked, "Why are you even here?"

Wade glanced at Lu and said, "He knows about the ketamine. If you don't play he's gonna turn us in to the cops."

Lu said, "Correction: if you don't win I'm going to turn you in to the cops. Consider that your cut." He grinned proudly at his evildoings and in his Confucius voice added, "The early bird may get the worm but the second mouse gets the cheese."

I slammed the door and went to check on Mom and Alicia. Mom's bathroom was locked. There were no sounds coming from the other side of the door except for the hiss of the steam bath. I guess I could have waited around to talk once they were done but that wasn't what anybody wanted. With a trip to Aspen looming in my future and a gut feeling I'd never be coming home again I decided to throw some clothes in a backpack and head for zee hills. I stopped the music and took the disk with me. Outside I stood at the end of our walk and faced our house. It looked just as normal as all the other homes on the block.

All I could think to do was hit golf balls. When I'm on the range I pretend I'm playing an imaginary golf course so it's a great escape. The range at the BGC was empty because a big storm was coming. Billowy, bright white thunderheads had gathered overhead and textured the landscape with shadows. Darker clouds loomed west of town and thunder rolled in from the mountains. The temperature had dropped and it wasn't even very late in the morning so we were in for a rainy day. That morning my fantasy golf course was at my fantasy boarding school and I played for the school's team in the final match of the season. I was doing pretty well until Pam arrived and ruined the dream.

She drove up in the drinks cart and said, "Melanie was just here asking questions about you. Guess they found your caddy bib right where her mom passed out naked? How could you?"

"How could I what?"

"Everyone knows the Vanleers can handle their booze, so what was in their Bloody Marys?"

"I dunno. You're the one who brought them the drinks."

"Something fishy's going on here and I'm gonna figure it out."

She left and the imaginary world I'd created was gone too so I packed it up and went to the bank and withdrew all my money. Between caddying and hustling over the years I had amassed over ten thousand dollars. The teller gave me a hundred hundred-dollar bills in a tidy stack held in place with a paper band that said $10,000 and I took the rest of the cash loose. I used the same bank Lu had his mortgage with because it was closest to the club and his broker Paul saw me at the counter and pulled me aside and told me to tell Lu to call him. He'd seen me in Lu's office and knew we were friends.

"How bad is it?" I asked him.

Paul shook his head. "Just see if you can get him to call me."

The rain started and I didn't know where to go or how to spend my day. I tried to think of what normal kids did the first week of their summer vacation and I didn't have a clue. I waited beneath the shelter of the bus stop with my bike and my backpack and to the rest of the world I probably looked like every other teenager, just like our house looked like every other house, but I was carrying around two changes of clothes and ten thousand dollars with nowhere to go so I didn't feel very normal.

A group of kids my age came running down the street to catch the bus and get out of the rain. There were four girls and two guys. None of them smoked or had nose rings or wore chains and black makeup. They were quiet even when they laughed. They got off the bus at the Walnut Street station so I did too and when they transferred to another bus I followed them. We rode east out of town on Route 36 and ten miles later they got off at the FlatIron Crossing mall so I did too. They didn't look at me twice and entered the shopping area through Nordstrom. I had to lock my bike and fell behind but spotted them a little later walking out of a Banana Republic. Then they went to J.Crew, then the Apple store, then Victoria's Secret, at which point the boys went across the promenade to Dick's Sporting Goods. Then they all met up in the food court in front of Old Navy. The girls got Jamba Juices and the boys got pizza so I got pizza too. I stood in line right behind them, which was the closest I'd been since riding the bus, and I worried that one of them would turn around and say, "Quit following us, freak."

I ate my slice a few tables down and listened to their banter about a clip on YouTube of a comedian I'd never heard of but they knew his routine by heart. Then they gossiped about some girl's profile picture on Facebook "that was taken like two years ago before she gained a thousand pounds." From there they discussed a romantic comedy the girls saw even though they knew it would suck, because they had nothing better to do. Without any kind of segue the next topic was the older brother of one of the guys who was in the army and stationed in Afghanistan. The girls thought he was hot. And finally they all griped about the summer jobs they were dreading to start, which made me reflect on my own line of work as Scam Artist.

I left them and wandered aimlessly until I passed one of the trendier clothing stores and saw a poster of Timmy Timmy Timmy in the window. He was shirtless in blue jeans and leaned against an old split-rail fence with a piece of hay in his mouth. I had to stop and laugh. Then I called him and on the first ring he answered, "Gator Gator, retaliator. Who're ya gettin' even with today today today?"

"I'm sorry about that call the other day. I was drunk, obviously."

"So what was the deal deal deal?"

"Oh, it's a long story."

"You're only seventeen, it can't be that long long long."

"Trust me, it's a doozy, and I really do want to explain but I'd rather wait and do it face-to-face."

"Face-to-face-face-face," he repeated thoughtfully. "Must be important important important."

"Dude, I know you've been waiting and honestly you're the best friend anyone could ever ask for and I promise when I lay it all out for you you'll understand."

He laughed and said, "Okay, you can explain later later later. So how's Mel and her mom's new twins twins twins?"

"Oh . . . we got drama."

He laughed and said, "Gator Gator, abominator."

"Where are you?"

"I'm about to get on a helicopter to fly out to the Hamptons Hamptons Hamptons."

"Helicopter? You're moving up in the world."

"The shoot is with an actress and the chopper's for her her her. She said she'd give me a ride ride ride."

"An actress? Is she famous?"

"Maybe, you'll just have to wait and see see see."

"What's the ad for?"

"If I tell you that then you'll know who it is is is."

"I don't like all these secrets," I told him.

"That's the pot calling the kettle black black black. Where are you you you?"

"I'm in the mall looking at your picture, cowboy."

He laughed and asked, "What are you doing at the mall mall mall?"

"I'm bored," I answered.

"You've been my best friend for four years years years. I've never once known you to be bored bored bored."

"Think of it as a step forward," I said.

"Definitely," he said, and hung up before he could stutter.

The group of kids I'd been tailing walked by and stared at the poster. One of the girls said, "Do you know that guy lives here in Boulder?"

Another girl said, "Yeah a friend of mine who goes to Boulder High knows him. She says he doesn't know how to talk or something. I guess he's pretty weird."

I turned to them and said, "He's not weird at all, he just gets kinda nervous."

They were all shocked I spoke. Two of the girls giggled and the group kept walking.

I went to the romantic comedy they talked about at lunch. It was just as bad as they said it was. Life as a regular kid seemed pretty boring and I wouldn't have wanted it any other way.

I took the bus back into town and rode my bike to Mel's house. Marty answered the door and greeted me with "Well if it isn't the man of the hour!" He laughed so hard he started to cough.

"Is Melanie home?" I asked.

"Oh, God no." He laughed some more and said, "Actually there's nothing funny about it!" He couldn't stop cracking up and sat on his fancy floor and buried his head between his knees while he slapped the imported and pampered wood with his palms in hysterics.

Mrs. Vanleer stepped around Marty onto the front porch and shut the door. "Sorry about that," she said.

"Is Melanie here?"

"Melanie won't talk to me. She's under the impression that you and I had sex. I tried to tell her I would never do such a thing and I'm fairly certain you wouldn't either although at the moment I'm a little suspicious after catching you spying on me in the laundry room."

"I wasn't spying on you," I said.

Mrs. Vanleer regarded me dubiously. "Melanie found me with my skirt pulled above my waist and your caddy bib beneath the very couch I had passed out on so you see how it looks suspicious. The other night when I hosted the dinner for the police one of the officers told me the biggest problem on campus these days is something called a date rape drug."

"Mrs. Vanleer," I pleaded.

She held up her hand and said, "Something's off here but we're going to figure it out. In the meantime do what you have to do to make this right for both our sakes." She went back inside and I stood on her front step and looked up and down the street that Mom said was one of the most desired locations in town.

I rode my bike through North Boulder's quaint little block of coffee shops and cafes and saw Ike, Sara and Wade eating at a sidewalk table. I straddled my bike and stared. Ike and Sara's ankles were intertwined beneath the table and they listened and laughed as Wade told them a story. I knew in that moment I had to go to Aspen and beat Ed in the match. Not to keep me and Wade out of jail, or to win Lu his money, but for Ike and Sara and the notion that good parents and normal families really can survive.

So I went to Harmony's Rest and got my blanket and pillow from behind the front desk and lay down on the couch in the common room. Melanie was somewhere out there hurting. She had given me so many reasons to love her and all I had given her was lies. I stared at the ceiling and realized I was no different than the person I had been the night before and the night before that. One good night's sleep hadn't been enough to change me and I had yet to have those difficult conversations. It's hard to bear one's soul through the crack of a bathroom door or to a car that's speeding away. Even so, I had spent the day like a bored, normal kid and it felt like a pretty good start.

towns can't hurt you

*t*he morning crew at Harmony's Rest woke me up at six and I went to North Boulder Park like every other morning. As usual the sky was blue in all directions and the sun had already dried what little moisture had accumulated overnight. I was the first person there and in the early morning silence tried to imagine what the day had in store. At noon Lu and I would drive to Jefferson County Airport, and from there a private jet would fly us to Aspen. I had never been on a plane before and was kinda afraid to fly but my mind was already filled with so much to feel anxious about that a crashing plane ranked near the bottom of the list.

The roller-skating woman appeared in the distance and walked toward me with a man. Her tights were black instead of pink and without her skates and big earphones she looked as normal as anyone else but it was nice to know an eccentric side of her existed. She smiled as they approached and discreetly waved her hand by her hip. They chatted merrily and didn't break their stride as they passed. I grinned and was certain she could feel my pleasure of seeing her with a friend. The men with the daughters arrived, coffee in hand, and their girls hopped out of the strollers and chased each other in circles. It had only been a few days since they'd taken their first steps and even though they were wobbly they were making it just fine on their own. Then the Down's boy with the dog zigzagged across the grass. His hair was wet and combed and he wore a clean collared shirt. I waved to him and he looked me in the eyes for half a second, which was long enough to see that he experienced moments of peace inside his unsettled shell. It felt like summer and this universal sense of harmony deluded me to believe one more attempt at an honest talk with Mom would actually work.

Right when I stood up from the bench to go home a car driving past the park backfired and the explosion from the exhaust pipe sounded like a gunshot. There'd never been a drive-by shooting in the city of Boulder so I didn't duck or flinch. I confidently walked toward the street on my way to find Mom, and was foolish enough to think there was nothing to fear.

Our street was quiet but there were a bunch of cars parked near Stuart's house and filling his driveway. Other than that, everything was normal. Bundled papers waited on stoops, lawns were mowed and sections of the sidewalk were wet from errant sprinklers. Somewhere a block or two over, a dog barked at the beeping sound a garbage truck made from being driven in reverse and the distant noise made our street seem all the more peaceful. Mom's car was parked next to Alicia's in our driveway, a sign the romance with Stuart had ended and I wondered what Alicia did this time to interfere.

Our house was empty and the kitchen counter was cluttered with a few empty bottles of Chardonnay, crumpled-up beer cans and two lipstick-smudged wineglasses. Mom's bedroom door was open and I stood completely still inside her room and tried to listen to the walls but they didn't speak. I wondered if my father really had built those walls like Alicia suggested. It was hard to imagine that somewhere out there existed a man responsible for our home's floor plan. There had to be better evidence than a putter hidden in the basement. I needed something damning like a picture or a love letter or a hate letter. Anything masculine and personal would suffice. A monogrammed handkerchief with the slightest scent of cologne would have been just as good as DNA.

I searched Mom's underwear drawer because people

hide their most intimate belongings in their underwear drawer. Everybody does it, which is why I hide my most prized possessions beneath my T-shirts. I didn't find any surprises but there was something Mom wasn't telling me and gut instinct sent me spying to Stuart's house. His blinds were down again but in one window the shades didn't quite reach the bottom and left a gap big enough to peek inside.

Stuart's living room had been transformed into a sex palace. Swings hung from the ceiling, human-sized cages occupied two corners and most of the floor space was covered with mattresses lying on platforms set at various heights. A disco ball had been knocked from its mounting and dangled precariously above a sleeping couple. Men and women in various states of undress were passed out everywhere. Mom, Alicia and Stuart slept on a mattress closest to the window. Mom was nude and her back was curled against Alicia's front. Alicia was only wearing panties and her back was curled against Stuart's front. Stuart was wearing some weird kind of sarong and cupped one of Alicia's silicone sacks as he slept.

I backed away from the window and sat on the lawn. I wished Lu was there to say something like *Man with tool in woman's mouth not necessarily dentist*, just to break the mood. But the truth is I didn't feel like laughing. I wasn't angry at Mom, nor was I very shocked. But I was angry at not being shocked. As a teenager it seemed my right to be entitled to a certain level of indignation at discovering my mother passed out at a swinger's party. But my mood flat-lined. Two years of Alicia's abuse along with the inescapable fear of Mom having another nervous breakdown had killed my emotional pulse. I wondered what the hell Melanie could possibly ever see in me and feared that sooner or later she'd realize I was nothing more than a tin man without any Oz.

I ran home to get my backpack and my bike. Mom had a small garden in our backyard she neglected. Special red bricks she bought at an antique shop bordered the perimeter. I removed the center brick, which left an unmissable gap. With white chalk I wrote on one side of the brick WEALLFU and on the other CKALICIA. Then I went to Stuart's and hurled it through the window in the direction of where they were sleeping.

I rode off while the window's shattering glass was still airborne and went straight to the Peterson's. It wasn't yet 7 A.M. but both Ike and Sara answered the door bright-eyed and neatly dressed. My uninvited presence at their home at such an early hour was bizarre but they were too gracious to show any kind of surprise to see me. Ike opened his front door wide and stepped aside as an invitation into his home. "Gates my man," he said all chipper. "What brings you to the hood?"

Sara had a tube of sunscreen in her hand and traces of unabsorbed zinc tinted her cheeks white. She smiled as she rubbed the lotion into her arms and casually said, "I think Wade is still asleep. Do you want me to wake him?" She looked at her watch, a neon green art deco inspired Swatch from the eighties, probably one of the few relics she held on to from that decade, and added, "He should probably be up already anyway."

"Let him sleep," I told her. "In fact, tell him not to come to work at all today."

Ike and Sara looked at each other, then Sara asked, "What do you mean?"

"Just tell him I'm not going to win tomorrow. He'll know what to do."

Ike and Sara were wise people; they'd been around the block enough times to know Wade was circling that same stretch of pavement. They thanked me and just before Ike closed the door he said, "Do what you gotta do man," and I felt better knowing the good guys were on my side.

Pam was not on my side and was waiting for me at the bag drop when I got to the golf club so I greeted her with "They teach you how to park cars in law school?"

She smirked as if she had sucked on a lemon. "I'm waiting for Wade."

"Ah. He should be here any second."

"Do you want to know why I'm waiting for Wade? Because if you drugged the Vanleers he was involved too. Everyone knows Wade's a dealer; you guys work the bag drop together; it all makes sense."

A car arrived so I said, "If you're gonna sit there you might as well help me unload the clubs." Pam didn't lift a finger. She waited two hours but Wade never showed. I still don't know where he is but Ike and Sara would go to the end of the earth to protect him so that's probably where they went.

Things slowed down around ten-thirty and Lu surfaced to find me. For our flight to Aspen he debuted a seersucker suit accessorized with a yellow ascot, white and tan saddle shoes and a vintage straw hat. I looked him over and said, "You look like you're dressed for a medicine show. Where's your snake oil?"

Lu brushed the lapels of his blazer proudly and replied, "I got tinctures."

"Why're you making me play this guy? We don't even know him and we're about to fly on his plane, stay at his house and play on his golf course and the whole thing's weird, man."

"It's odd, but the guy's got a hard-on for you Gator. You seem to have that effect on a lot of middle-aged men, Fun Buns."

"And you keep dangling me in front of them, don't ya?"

Lu palmed the top of his straw hat and held it behind his back. "Prepare yourself for Lu's Amazing Adventures!"

"It's bunk, dude."

"It's an easy fifty grand."

"I wouldn't be so sure. I got a lot on my mind right now so don't expect me to bring my A game."

Lu held his hat out to the side and tried to flip it onto his head with a flourish but missed and it fell to the ground. He picked the hat up and said, "Win or jail, that'll get your A game going."

"You'd really have me arrested?"

Lu shrugged. "Just win and we won't have to find out." He wrapped his palm around the back of my neck and nudged me toward the clubhouse. "Go and get your clubs. There's a man in Aspen waiting to see you about a game of golf."

I pushed his hand off me and said, "You're making a mistake. Seriously."

Lu shook his head and wagged his finger. Like Confucius he said, "Babies in the dark make mistakes. Mistakes in the dark make babies."

That was the moment when I began to suspect Ed's motivations. Life is funny like that. I mean Lu's stupid jokes were always so annoying I never thought one would actually make me think.

I ran to the pro shop and called Melanie's house. She

answered the phone and I said, "Mel, you're never gonna believe it."

"Not if it comes out of your mouth."

"Seriously, this is kinda major."

"I'll tell you what's major. Pam is in my living room right now telling my parents you and Wade drugged them."

"Pam wants a job from your dad. She'd tell him she could shit gold bricks if she thought it would get her hired."

"Yeah well they're thinking about calling the police. Dad wants to wait until Monday because we're about to hit the road to Aspen for the Food & Wine Festival and he's in some bizarre rush to get there by five but Mom is freaking out because she thinks you might have raped her."

"Raped her? Come on Mel, you know I wouldn't do that."

"You lied about being there and you lied about a bunch of other things too."

"I didn't lay a finger on your mom but thanks for the double standard."

"What double standard?"

"The one that says it's okay for your dad to fondle my ass but if your mom suspects the same of me she calls the cops."

"You're really gonna blame this on Dad? He likes you Gates. Maybe he gets a little too friendly but has he ever got you so drunk you woke up hours later with your pants around your ankles and couldn't remember what happened?"

"Your parents had been up all night drinking and you know that. By the time they got to the golf course they were already tanked but thanks for sticking up for me." I snorted and added, *"Maybe he gets a little too friendly* . . . I love how you make it sound so innocent."

"Why'd you lie about being in the den with them?"

"I don't know. It was stupid."

"Did you drug them or not?"

"Look, I'm about to head up to Aspen too, for a golf game, but I really wanted to tell you something."

"A *golf game*?" She tsk'd loudly. "I love how you make it sound so innocent. Do me a favor: if you see me up in Aspen this weekend turn around and walk the other way." She hung up and though I was disheartened at least she had said she loved something about me. Her sentiment dripped with sarcasm and spite but it was all I had to hang on to and I wasn't about to let it go.

Lu walked into the office and tapped his watch. "Let's boogie, Chawlie," he said in a ridiculous Chinese accent.

"You wanna go now? We'll be half an hour early."

In another performance of Confucius he replied, "Man who throw clock watch time fly." He grinned and flicked his eyebrows.

"See, now I know you're nervous," I said. "You know just as well as me this is a bad idea and that's why you keep making those dumb Confucius jokes, because that's what you do when you get nervous."

"I make them all the time."

"I know, because you're always insecure and uncomfortable. Look at how you're dressed: we're going to Aspen not the Ozarks."

Lu actually seemed hurt. He looked down and said, "Jeez, what'd I do?"

"You know exactly what you're doing and you know it's lame. That's why you're acting this way." I hoisted my backpack over my shoulder. "Now if you want me to play in this stupid match you're gonna have to carry my clubs to the car."

I headed out to the parking lot and a few minutes later Lu appeared with my sticks. It was a small victory but it was one to grow on. I thought about not going and calling his bluff to see if he'd really have me arrested. I wanted to believe he wouldn't. I wanted to believe that just beneath his ill-conceived natty veneer was someone I could count on. But it wasn't even noon and I'd already been naive enough for one day. I was also a little worried about the Vanleers calling the cops and so jetting out of town didn't seem like such a bad idea. I had over ten thousand dollars in my backpack, a mother having threesomes with my godmother and our neighbor, and a girlfriend who right-fully knew me only as a liar. I looked around the parking lot and wanted to believe it would somehow all go away but that was a fairy tale. And then there was Ed and my theory on why he wanted to play me in golf and that too seemed equally far-fetched. So I grasped even tighter to Mel's mocking testament of love for me and relished even harder my tiny triumph over Lu. The only option left was to willfully surrender to the world of make-believe Lu called his Amazing Adventure. I may have been nothing more than a tin man, but at least I had found an Oz.

Lu and I got to the airport forty-five minutes early. The terminal was a small waiting room with nice carpeting and wood-paneled walls. Coffee, bottled water and pastries were set out for free. Lu sat on a couch on one side of the building and I took a seat as far away from him as possible. We were the only people there but I didn't wanna risk being seen with a guy wearing an ascot. Stacks of a maga-zine about how wealthy Coloradans lived were distributed to every corner of the room. The pages were filled with pic-tures of rich people at parties. There wasn't one article longer than three paragraphs. I stared back and forth be-tween Lu and the photographs of the well-to-do and he didn't look that different all gussied up in his seersucker suit but he didn't quite fit in either. And that was all he wanted, to be what he imagined was a better version of himself, so in that respect we were no different, especially since we were both failing miserably.

I flipped through the society rag. A lot of the party pictures were taken in Aspen and when the reality finally hit me I'd be there in less than an hour I walked across the room and sat down next to Lu and said, "I can't do this."

Lu must have seen the trepidation in my eyes because he very compassionately asked, "What's the matter?"

"When I was fifteen my mom tried to kill herself and got sent to an asylum so I was sent to live with my godmother in Aspen and while I was there something really bad happened and I don't want to go back there. For real."

"It's just a town. Towns can't hurt you."

"I'm not gonna feel comfortable there Lu. There's no way I'll have my swing."

"You're gonna play just fine. You always do."

"This is different."

Lu's gaze had a softness I didn't know he possessed. "Tell me then, what was so bad that happened to you?"

"She kissed me. She was supposed to take care of me and she kissed me while my mom was locked away somewhere I couldn't even find her."

Lu burst out with laughter. "She kissed you!" Like a rowdy Confucius he said, "Passionate kiss like spiderweb; soon lead to undoing of fly!"

"You're a jerk."

"Oh please! I've seen your godmother. There isn't a fif-teen-year-old boy who wouldn't want to put his hands all over her big beautiful dumplings."

"Except for maybe her godson," I said.

Lu thought about it. He shook his head and said, "No, him too."

"Well I tried to run away, you know why? Because it was wrong."

He howled as if my story was ridiculous and shouted in his Confucius voice, "If sex is a pain in the ass you're doing it wong!"

"Go ahead and laugh but it messed me up good and you're about to take me right back to the lion's den and I'm warning you now there's a good chance I'm gonna lose my shit and all your money in the process because hon-estly Lu, the threat of going to jail doesn't even come close to rivaling the trauma and demons Aspen represents to me."

The tone of my voice caught Lu's attention and I think he actually considered backing out but then Ed's large jet landed on the runway with a thunderous roar and the sight of such an elegant and elite status symbol was too much for Lu to refuse.

flowerpots and
underwear drawers

a perky blonde named Piper greeted us in Aspen. The terminal was filled with people but she walked right up to me and said, "You must be Gates." When I asked how she knew she seemed embarrassed and replied, "I don't know. Lucky guess I guess." Piper was Ed's "ambassador." She was young enough to be his daughter but I'm pretty sure her "ambassadorial" duties required they not be related by blood. She led us outside, where two guys loaded my clubs from the back of a cart into a black Mercedes SUV. Lu climbed in the backseat like a man accustomed to being chauffeured and I hopped in front. We headed south toward town on Route 82 and then turned left onto Cemetery Lane. My stomach flipped because Alicia's house was on Cemetery Lane.

"Where're we headed?" I asked.

"Starwood. Know where that is?"

"Yeah, I lived here for a year. Right on this road actually." I said this as we passed Alicia's house and Piper looked right at it as if she already knew. I waited for her to inquire what circumstances brought me to spend a year in her town but she didn't ask, which wasn't very ambassadorial of her. After a moment of silence I asked, "So how long have you been Ed's ambassador?"

"About a year."

"That's a unique title. I don't think I've ever known anyone who had a personal ambassador."

"Ed's a unique guy." She grinned at the mention of his name the way I hoped Melanie would smile when she said my name.

"Yeah, I played golf with him and a woman named Paula a few days ago. They were both pretty unique if you ask me."

Piper laughed. "Those two are quite a pair, that's for sure."

"So where is he?"

"In Houston at a board meeting for an oil company. He'll be back for dinner." She kept her eyes on the road as we crossed a narrow bridge and passed a parking lot for a bike trail along a river.

"Does he always fly people in for golf matches?"

"Not always."

"Why me?"

Piper kept her eyes on the road as we switchbacked up a hill and I let her concentrate but when the terrain flattened out she still didn't speak. After a few miles we turned into a gated entrance and headed down a long driveway through a rugged mountain property surrounded by a white post fence. The terrain alternated between open fields of long grass and thick hilly pockets of aspens and pines. Eventually we arrived at a stone and wood shingled mansion with huge tinted glass windows that overlooked the valley. Piper told me to leave my clubs in the car and walked Lu and me to a similarly styled guesthouse on the far end of a large swimming pool area that stretched out from the rear of the main house. She told us to take a few minutes to freshen up and then we'd head to Ed's course for a practice round.

Lu was fired up and changed into a white and turquoise linen ensemble but I told him he couldn't come because he'd be a distraction, especially in that outfit. He wanted to win so badly he actually agreed to stay behind. "What do you think an ambassador does?" He asked as if he was considering getting one of his own.

"Who knows. She's probably his secretary, or maybe his girlfriend, or both."

Like Confucius Lu replied, "Secretary not permanent until screwed on desk."

"You sound like a moron," I told him and left the guest-house with my backpack because I didn't trust leaving Lu alone near all my money.

Piper and I set off to Ed's course sans Lu and she asked about the flight and what the weather was like in Boulder that morning and if I was excited to be in Aspen. She was much more talkative without Lu around but still picked her words carefully. We had to drive back down Cemetery Lane to get to the highway and when we approached Alicia's house I asked her to pull into the driveway. She could have kept driving but she didn't and that alone won me over.

Alicia bought her house twenty years ago when she moved to Colorado from Ohio. Back then all the homes on her street were ski shacks inhabited by locals but time and trend shifted the demographics of the block into a neighborhood of vacation homes. Alicia moved to Boulder ten years ago after she met Mom at some hippy-dippy women's retreat in Santa Fe. She put the house in Aspen to work as a rental property, then remodeled and eventually became such a successful shrink she didn't need the extra money and started using the home again on weekends.

I hopped out of Piper's car and nervously looked down the street because Mom and Alicia were on their way. They never missed the Food & Wine Festival and they could have left Boulder extra early after being woken by a flying brick. I wandered to Alicia's backyard. The bushes and the grass were overgrown but the hot tub was clean and warm. Piper checked the water's temperature and sarcastically remarked, "I guess she has her priorities straight."

"Who's that?"

"The owner of this house."

"How do you know she's a she?"

"It doesn't really matter if it's a he or a she; we aren't supposed to be here."

I walked to the corner of the deck and grabbed the house key Alicia always hid beneath a clay green and white striped flowerpot she had painted herself. "You ever notice there're basically two hiding places in the world? The back of underwear drawers and beneath flowerpots."

Piper stared at the key in my hand and said, "Put it back."

"Wanna know another good hiding spot? Aspen." I unlocked the door and stepped inside; Piper followed. "This house is one big underwear drawer . . ." I spun around quickly and said, "You know exactly who lives here, so what else do you know?"

Piper looked around the entrance and said, "I know we shouldn't be doing this."

"Breaking and entering or having this conversation?"

"Both."

"Now you're telling me something."

We walked back to the car and I said, "Let's go into town. I don't feel like playing golf."

"What about your match?"

"If my match is really just about a golf game take me to the course. If it's about something else then I don't want to practice for a charade."

When we reached the highway Piper turned left toward town, the opposite direction of Ed's course, and smiled with gleeful satisfaction from breaking rules she didn't believe. I said to her, "Thank you for being honest."

Piper kept a straight face and replied, "What? I just wanna get some ice cream."

She valeted the car at the Little Nell hotel and bought me an ice-cream cone at Paradise Bakery. We sat in Ruby Park and people-watched. It had only been two years since I'd been to Aspen and I remembered the town being filled with sturdy citizens who wore Patagonias and flip-flops but all the men who walked by were metrosexuals and the women were painted and plastic and wore bedazzled designer sweatsuits and sandals with enormous wedge-shaped heels. Piper was dressed in khaki L.L.Bean hiking shorts, a plain white T-shirt and dirty trail shoes that made me like her even more.

She wanted to take the gondola to the top of Ajax and we rode up the mountain with a couple from France or Germany or some Euro-type place. The guy's shirt was ambitiously unbuttoned to his waist and the woman pouted and snapped pictures every other second with a snazzy pink camera. There were a few sections of the ride where the gondola was suspended hundreds of feet in the air and the wind blew the carriage back and forth like a big plastic pendulous egg. The woman squealed every time we got too high and the guy responded to each shriek with *"Zut,"* which must be Euro for "Zip it." I wanted to ask him if everyone in his country hid their valuables in underwear drawers and their house keys beneath planters but didn't want to be *Zut'*d so I guess I'll never know.

At the top of the mountain we could see in every direction for hundreds of miles. I looked northeast and knew that somewhere out there Melanie and Mom were headed in my direction. Piper and I had lunch on the sundeck and sat in cozy recliners and talked for hours. Piper told me all about herself. She was born in Rumson, New Jersey, and went to college in Vermont. Her parents were still married after thirty years. She believed in everlasting love and she believed in Ed but when I pressed for more info about him she wouldn't go there and I respected her for being an adult and minding other people's boundaries.

We caught the last gondola down and I led us to a souvenir shop that sold every useless knickknack they could fit the word *Aspen* on and bought two postcards, one for 3T's and one for the roller-skater woman. 3T's card showed a blonde skiing in a bikini and said, "How's your Aspen?" On the back I wrote, *By the time you get this everyone will know I've been sleeping with my godmother.* The card for the skater was a beautiful picture of the Maroon Bells mountain range. On the back I wrote *Suite #7.* I stamped both and dropped them in a mailbox so there was no turning back. Piper had no idea what the cards were about but her patience suggested she knew they were important. At the end of the day we returned to get her car at the Little Nell and while we were standing beneath the hotel's covered entrance waiting for the valet the Vanleers' car sped down Durant Street straight toward us. I turned to Piper and calmly said, "Pardon me," then sprinted inside.

The lobby of the Little Nell is attached to a sunken sitting room that looks out on a patio and swimming pool. The area is flanked by two bars and is a popular après-ski spot in the winter. Alicia took me there a few times when we lived in town. She'd get a glass of wine for her and a beer for me and we'd sit in the lounge and stare at the big fire sipping our drinks like we were on some kind of date. No one noticed I was underage and drinking beer even though the only reason people were there was to ogle everyone. In the spring and summer the scene moves to the outdoor deck upstairs where the gondola loads and offloads so when I ran inside to hide from the Vanleers the room was empty except for a father and his young daughter even though it was happy hour.

The dad was in his thirties and definitely not from Colorado. He had a crisp boyish haircut and leather shoes with tassels. His shorts and oxford shirt still had iron creases even though it was the end of the day. He couldn't take his eyes off his BlackBerry and sighed as he pecked at the keyboard. His movements were sharp and aggravated. He was exactly the kind of guy I never felt badly about hustling. His little girl had a brand-new cast on her leg and she sat by sullenly and kicked his white canvas bag that said *Goldman Sachs* with her good leg.

"Don't," the dad said.

She'd stop and as soon as he got back to his BlackBerry she'd start again.

"Ashley! I mean it."

"Why can't we find Mom?" she asked.

"I don't know. Make sure you ask her that when we do find her."

"Where is she?"

"Not where she said she'd be."

The girl kicked the bag again and said, "I can't believe I broke my leg and she didn't even come to the hospital."

"I'm sure there's a good reason," the father said, but then he muttered, "There better be."

I sat in an armchair that faced the front desk and hid

behind a newspaper. Piper came in and took the seat next to me. A second later Marty charged through the door. He looked at his watch and sped to the concierge. Mrs. Vanleer and Melanie trailed him. They weren't smiling the way people usually do when they arrive at a hotel and seemed most concerned with staying out of Marty's way.

Piper whispered, "Who are they?"

"My girlfriend and her parents," I whispered back.

Piper said, "She's cute," and got up and walked in between Melanie and Mrs. Vanleer and stood right next to Marty as he checked in. I couldn't watch.

The girl with the broken leg had blond pigtails, blue eyes and a little ski jump nose. She gazed around the lobby with a well-practiced boredom that suggested she'd spent many hours waiting on her mother. Her father checked his BlackBerry again. She watched his frustration grow and grinned.

Piper returned and whispered, "The parents are staying in room 214 and the girl's in 307." Marty handed key cards to Mrs. Vanleer and Melanie and shoved some money into a bellhop's hand, then quickly headed for the door. Piper said, "There's only one thing that can make a man that impatient," and then went off after him.

On her way out Piper passed a skinny blond woman in black spandex tights, a stretchy black long-sleeve shirt zipped up her neck, a black baseball hat and those big black sunglasses that make women look like insects. She was probably attractive but it was hard to tell. Her legs were so skinny the spandex hung loose from her calves, which wasn't all that hot, but she looked like she always smelled good and probably wore sexy underwear. She headed straight for the little girl and the dad quickly stood to greet her. "Jesus Christ Gervaise!"

Before she even acknowledged her injured daughter the woman hissed at her husband, "Do you know how many of my friends left me a voicemail telling me you called them looking for me like some kind of maniac?"

"Where were you?"

"You managed to only offend half of them so at least that's an improvement."

"You told me you were going for a hike with Fernanda."

"And after you called her you called about a hundred other people, didn't you?"

"Our daughter broke her leg and no one could find you."

"And thanks to you now everybody knows."

"Fernanda didn't remember your plans to hike. So I called Vandy and she said she saw you at the tennis courts but when I called the club they said you hadn't been there all day. Moral of the story is Vandy's a better friend."

The little girl with the broken leg kicked the canvas bag absentmindedly and waited for one of her parents to say that if she had been more careful none of this would have happened in the first place. That was the road in front of her and that was the weight she would carry and the dulled apathetic look in her eyes suggested that even at her young age she had already come to understand and accept this fate.

Piper returned ten minutes later and plopped down on her chair and said, "Whoa . . . didn't see that one coming."

"Let me guess," I said. "He met a man in a coffee shop and they quickly left together."

Piper shook her head. "Nope. The guy was parked around the corner waiting for him. He hopped in the car and they drove off like they'd just robbed a bank. How'd you know?"

"Thanks to him my nickname at the golf course is Fun Buns."

Piper nodded sagely and replied, "Well it looks like your buns are safe for now." She winked and like Mel she could pull off the gesture without looking dopey.

I got an idea and said, "I'll be back in a bit," and ran upstairs.

Melanie's mother had hung a DO NOT DISTURB sign on her door and I had to knock a bunch of times until she answered in one of the hotel's terry cloth robes. She very coolly stepped aside to let me into the room and rehung the sign and closed the door. Thick curtains blocked the windows and the only source of light came from candles flickering in the bathroom. The lower fringes of Mrs. Van-leer's hair were wet and the top of her head was dry. She gathered the damp portion behind her neck and flipped up the collar of her robe. "I know you drugged me, Gates. Pam told us this morning that you probably put GHB in my drink. The only reason I didn't call the police was because Melanie talked me out of it."

"I didn't give you GHB."

"Well we'll find out for sure on Monday when I get a toxicology report."

"I gave you ketamine. Marty too."

"What in the good Lord's name is ketamine?"

"An animal tranquilizer."

"And why on heaven's earth would you do such a thing?"

"Because your husband sexually assaults me on a daily basis and no one seems to notice or care so I decided to get him back."

"By sexually assaulting me?"

"I didn't touch you. You touched you just like you were doing in the bathtub a minute ago when I knocked on the door."

Mrs. Vanleer tightened her robe and peered over her shoulder toward the bathroom.

"I'm in love with Melanie," I told her. "I'd never betray her like that."

"It looks very suspicious. Especially since you lied about being in the den with us."

"I didn't touch you and I need to know you won't involve the police."

"That's something I'll have to discuss with Marty. He's not going to be very forgiving when he learns you slipped him a tranquilizer."

"Do you know where Marty is right now?" I asked her.

Her eyes never left mine as she carefully chose her words, "You're in no position to be asking questions."

"What position do you think Marty's in? Because we both know he's with another man right now. I wonder what all your friends at the club would say about that?"

"They'd say you're a sad little boy and then you'd be fired."

"And then I'd find his barely legal masseur and get him and his waxed chest to tell everyone about Marty's happy endings in the guest room by the laundry."

We stared at each other in a heated silence. Everything in the dim room was perfectly still except for the shadows of the flickering candles in the bathroom. I wondered if it was possible for Mrs. Vanleer to have any more epiphanies or if her life was too far gone for change. Then she said, "All this from the boy who supposedly loves our daughter."

I nodded and answered, "Right to her mother who stripped for him."

Mrs. Vanleer sat on the edge of her bed and dropped her head into her hands. After a few deep breaths she looked up and said, "I've never been more ashamed in my entire life. It'd been so long since I'd undressed in front of anyone other than Marty and knowing that you'd been staring at my bathing suit by the pool excited me so I guess I was just looking for a little cheap thrill. I honestly thought it'd be harmless because I really didn't know you could see me."

"I wasn't looking," I said.

"That's a lie," she said.

"I'm in love with your daughter, Mrs. Vanleer. Whaddaya want me to say?"

She rubbed her temples with her palms and asked, "What's happened to me? I used to be a good mother, didn't I?"

"You did."

"How did I fall so far so fast?" She threw her arms up in desperation and said, "I'm sorry. You're just a boy. I shouldn't be dumping all this on you."

The apology won me over. For that brief moment the woman in crisis reverted back to the sensible parent I had always known. I wondered how long she would stay. "You need to work things out with Mr. Vanleer," I said.

"Trying to fix my marriage would be like trying to get toothpaste back in the tube."

"Then get a new tube."

"You mean a divorce?" She laughed and shook her head. "I can't think that big right now. What I want is a distraction." She shrugged and added, "Go ahead and judge me but I'm only being honest."

"You're a beautiful woman. A lot of men would love to be with you."

She laughed hopelessly and replied, "I wouldn't even know where to start."

"You should start with what you want," I said. "Does your cell phone have a camera? A friend of mine has a crush on you. Let's send him some pictures."

"Pictures! Gates this is ridiculous!"

"If Marty can have fun why can't you? Besides, you said all you want is a cheap thrill and if I know Timmy Timmy Timmy in a few minutes he'll be texting you back."

"Timmy the model?" She grimaced and shook her head. "Absolutely not. This is preposterous. He's just a boy too and I'm not about to commit the same sin twice."

"What if he sent you some pictures first? Then he'd be asking for it."

She quickly rattled off her phone number and locked herself in the bathroom. I didn't get a definitive word about whether she'd press charges against me for the drink spiking but she brought her phone to the bathtub so there was still a way to keep me from justice.

I called 3T's from the hallway right outside her room and he answered, "Gator Gator, deliberator. What's on your mind today my friend friend friend?"

"Well it's funny you should ask," I said.

3T's was jazzed up and I'm not sure he even heard the gravity of my voice because he talked right over me and asked, "Hey, have you ever heard of a golf club called Shinnecock Shinnecock Shinnecock? We just finished a shoot on the deck of their clubhouse clubhouse clubhouse. "

"You're at Shinnecock right now? Damn you."

"I thought you'd be jealous jealous jealous."

I could see his grin from two thousand miles away and I hated to rain on his parade but this was an emergency. "I'm about to text you a phone number," I told him. "Can you send some pictures of yourself to it?"

He laughed and joked, "Are you selling my pictures on the internet again again again?"

"It's Mrs. Vanleer's number."

Silence.

I continued: "See if you can get her to send you some pictures of herself back. The more revealing the better."

"What kind of sick shit are you up to to to?"

"I'll explain later but it might just keep me out of jail."

Timmy Timmy Timmy sighed into the phone, once, and asked, "When when when?"

"Now?"

"I'm at a super-private golf club and they've had people watching us like hawks all day day day. What am I supposed to do do do?"

"Go into a stall in the bathroom and take your shirt off and do that magical model thing." I hoped he'd laugh. He didn't.

"I'll do my best but no promises promises promises."

"If anyone can do it Timmy Timmy Timmy can," I said cheerfully but he didn't think anything about our conversation was funny. "I sent you a postcard today that'll make this seem tame," I said because I desperately wanted to hear him laugh.

"My mom is forwarding me all my mail so I'm sure she'll find it interesting interesting interesting," he replied with utter disgust. "Get it together man, you're too cool to be this fucked up." They were the meanest and kindest words he'd ever spoken to me and he didn't stutter.

"I'm trying the best I can."

"You'll get there, you're Gator Gator Gator." He hung up and I felt like the luckiest heel in the world.

I rode the elevator to the lobby and met Piper. The elevator next to mine opened at the same time and out walked Gervaise, her husband and their little girl with the broken leg. Gervaise's jeans were somehow tighter than the black spandex pants she had on earlier and she wore six-inch heels that made her taller than her spouse. She was much prettier in street clothes and brimmed with a confidence that suggested no matter where she went or who she was with she was always in charge. Her husband had a terse look on his face and reluctantly held her hand. The little girl hobbled behind them on crutches. She had cut out a Prada label from one of her mom's pieces of clothes and taped it to the top of the cast. A bellhop trailed them with a large and small duffel bag on a baggage cart.

Piper and I followed them outside, where a black Lincoln Navigator with the hotel's name stenciled on both sides waited. The bellhop loaded the bags in the back as Gervaise pecked the little girl's forehead goodbye. Piper's car was still parked by the door from when the valet first brought it up but I didn't hop in. When Piper realized I wasn't coming she walked back to me and said, "Come on, we gotta pick up Ed at the airport."

"Take Lu instead. He can be my ambassador."

"Just give him a chance, Gates. He's already convinced you'll never forgive him."

Gervaise watched the Navigator drive away and then headed in our direction. As she passed I said to her, "Excuse me, but are all sins forgivable?"

She stopped abruptly and actually thought for a moment before she replied, "Forgiveness is a skill. All the happy people I know have that skill. The unhappy ones don't."

"Should a child forgive a parent who abandons them?"

Very confidently she answered, "Yes."

"What about a parent or godparent who molests a child? Should the child forgive that too?"

With the same conviction as her first answer Gervaise replied, "Yes. It's the only way to move on. But the hardest person to forgive is yourself. That's where the real work is."

Piper was quiet as we drove away. To break the tension I joked, "Advice from an adulterer," but her hands shook against the steering wheel and tears were in her eyes. "Not all fun and games, is it?" I said.

"You know," her voice quivered, "I've already said too much and should really just stay out of this."

"If you don't mind, drop me off at Cemetery Lane. If Ed wants to have dinner with me then I need his help with something first."

When we reached Alicia's street Piper pulled over and I hopped out with my backpack. She shook her head and pleaded with her eyes for me not to make such a request of Ed. That's when I knew for sure he was my father.

paradise rules

I walked down Cemetery Lane slowly and stopped many times along the way to gather my thoughts and give Piper and Ed a chance to catch up to me. When I reached Alicia's her car was in the driveway and her trunk was still open so she and Mom had either just pulled in or were too absentminded to close the hatch. I snuck around the side of the house and spied them having a drink on the deck. Mom looked out at the rolling top of Buttermilk ski area from the edge of the deck. Her sagging posture suggested either something heavy was on her mind or she was merely hungover. Life with her and Alicia was always impossible to unscramble. The setting sun cast long jagged shadows down the face of the slope. Alicia wrapped her arm around Mom's waist and Mom leaned her head against Alicia's shoulder and cupped Alicia's butt with her free hand, which initiated a kiss too passionate for me to watch but explicit enough to decode.

I crept to the front of the house and waited for Ed. He was my smoking gun and would make it impossible for Mom to lie about if she was in Arizona the year I spent in Aspen or in Boulder with him. The Roaring Fork River ran between the airport and Ed's house so the only way for him to get home was to drive over the bridge at the bottom of Cemetery Lane so he had no choice but to head my way. The temperature dropped along with the sinking sun but still no Ed. I waited and waited and then Alicia opened the front door and was so surprised to find me she shrieked and dropped her wineglass, which shattered on the ground. She scowled at me and said, "What are you doing here? You scared the living daylights out of me." There was a bandage above her left eye.

"What happened to your forehead?"

"Someone hurled a brick through a window this morning and it landed on my face. I had to get seven stitches."

I raised my eyebrow in mock surprise and replied, "Wow. Will it leave a scar?"

"Probably."

"Guess that makes us even then."

From inside Mom yelled, "Alicia? What's going on?" We heard her footsteps running toward us and when she saw me she froze.

A black Mercedes SUV headed down Cemetery Lane and when the car got close I said, "Mom, Alicia and I had sex the entire year we lived in this house and she told me you were never in the hospital in Arizona but actually living in Boulder with this man!" I pointed at the SUV, which I thought would pull into the driveway, but the car didn't stop. All eyes followed the black Mercedes. Piper was driving and blocked the view of Ed. We watched the vehicle until it rounded a bend and went out of sight. Mom looked back and forth from me to where the car had disappeared and said, "I need a drink," and went back inside.

Alicia grabbed my wrist hard. "Trust me, you don't want to take this any further."

I ran after Mom to the kitchen. She was drinking wine from the bottle. There was a puddle around her glass on the counter so she must have tried to pour a drink but her hand was too shaky. "Where do you want to start?" I asked her.

Alicia came running into the room and Mom held up her hand and said, "Give us a minute, okay?"

Alicia pointed at me and replied, "I have the right to defend myself if he's going to make ridiculous claims about me."

"I know," Mom said. "I know, I know, I know!" She scowled at me and Alicia. "I did my best to look away because I knew I deserved it but haven't I paid enough?"

"I knew it," I sneered.

Alicia grabbed Mom's hand and tried to hug her but Mom pushed her away and hissed at her, "Don't act so surprised. You wanted me to know."

"Not in a million years," Alicia replied, and when she realized how deceptive it sounded she added, "I knew how much it would hurt you."

"But that's exactly what you wanted," Mom said. "What other motivation could you have possibly had for sleeping with your girlfriend's son?" With a bitter laugh she sarcastically suggested, "True love?"

"Hey!" Alicia spat back, "I raised him while you walked all over me so watch what you say!"

"You knew how confused I was," Mom said. "How could you?"

"When are you not confused?" Alicia asked her. "Stuart's the perfect example."

Mom sneered and replied, "And then you went and did it again, didn't you?" She shook her head with disgust. "Jesus, Alicia . . . he's just a boy."

"So how long have you known, anyway?" I asked bitterly.

Mom tried to slice me in half with a nasty stare and said, "Oh take off the halo, Gates. You were just as angry at me as she was. Why else would you guys have sex in the middle of the morning with the bedroom door wide open while I'm sitting in the kitchen trying to eat my breakfast?

You didn't think I could hear you guys the other day? Give me a break."

Alicia said, "That wasn't my idea; he practically raped me."

Mom flung a shockingly hard slap across Alicia's face and Alicia bowed her head. They both looked at me with such blame I felt like the little girl in the hotel with the broken leg. I looked at Mom through different eyes that no longer saw her as fragile. She was the alpha dog, tall, blond and beautiful, just like Gervaise.

"How come you never said anything?" I asked her.

"More guilt?" she replied sarcastically. "Really? From you? I'm sorry but wasn't I the one who was so torn between following my heart and giving you a proper upbringing that I literally tried to kill myself because the choice was too hard to make?" She grabbed Alicia's hand and continued: "And then when I sacrificed the greatest love in my life to do the quote-unquote right thing how does my son pay me back? By sleeping with the very woman I abandoned to give him a better life! So do I forgive myself? No. I think I'll always regret being so incredibly stupid!"

Alicia threw her arms around Mom and said, "I'm sorry. It was an agonizing time for all of us."

"I was fifteen years old," I said.

And Alicia said, "I caught you masturbating in my bed with my underwear so don't play the victim."

"That's because you walked around the house naked every day! What'd you expect?"

Alicia dropped her jaw with indignation and said, "Well I didn't expect you to start kissing me!"

"That's exactly what you expected!" I pointed back and forth between her and Mom and said, "Now it all makes sense. Mom left you for my dad so you decided to get back at her or make her jealous by being with me! You're even crazier than I thought!" To Mom I said, "You know she actually had me pull out her tampon. That's when I tried to run away but I bet she never told you about that, did she?"

Alicia said, "I am not going to stand here and be sabotaged with such outrageous lies."

Mom covered her ears and turned her head.

"I was fifteen!" I shouted. "Will somebody please acknowledge that?"

"You were constantly spying on me and doing disgusting things with my underwear," Alicia said. "You're a sex maniac. You forced yourself on me the other morning. You masturbated on your mother's bed. You're constantly sneaking around spying on us. So don't paint me the pervert. You did nothing against your will."

"I had just hit puberty," I said. "I didn't even have a will."

"Don't say you didn't want me," she said.

"But I didn't want you. I tried to run away in the

middle of a blizzard so that we wouldn't have sex, remember?"

"You mean after you groped me Halloween night and then pleasured yourself on my bed the next morning? You're telling two different stories Gates and quite frankly we don't believe either of them."

Mom shook her head and asked me, "How could you do this to us?"

"I didn't even know you guys were girlfriends," I said.

Alicia pulled Mom closer and said, "The sooner we put this behind us the sooner we can move forward."

"It's okay," Mom replied softly. "It's over."

"It's over?" I asked angrily. "I have to live with this for the rest of my life. It'll never be over, that's the point."

Mom shook her head and said, "If we can all agree to move on, then it's over."

"I didn't come here to sweep this under a carpet," I said.

"Why did you come here?" Alicia asked with a tone.

"Because I'm an idiot," I answered. "I actually thought you guys might want to talk about this like rational, sensitive people and we could all somehow get healed."

"Well I think we just did," Mom said. She was honestly ready to drop the whole subject and never look back and it made me want to punch her in the face.

Instead I replied, "Not even close," and headed for the door.

Mom caught up to me on the front steps and asked, "Who were you pointing at in the car that just drove by?"

"No one. I was bluffing. And I left the note in Stuart's mailbox last week, not Alicia." They were the most generous lies I've ever told. Paradise Rules.

Mom seethed with anger and gasped, "You little bastard. I'll never forgive you."

"Then you'll never be happy."

"I'll be happy when you're gone."

"You could have sent me to boarding school last year."

"Believe me I wanted to, but Alicia talked me out of it."

I let the words hang and then sarcastically asked, "Hmm, I wonder why?"

"I wish I never had you."

"At least you didn't waste a lot of energy loving me."

Mom snorted and replied, "Oh, grow up already."

I smiled and said, "Tell Stuart I'm sorry about his window." I walked away but then turned around and added, "On second thought, have Alicia tell him for me. She can do it the next time he's fucking her." I raised my arm up and waved like a friendly neighbor, and those were the last words I ever spoke to my mother.

I went back to the Little Nell and booked a room. The concierge told me they'd been completely booked but had just gotten a cancellation that evening, which must have been the room belonging to the little girl with the broken leg. It seemed fitting we'd share this space and made me feel better about my decision to stay there. The hotel was very expensive and I charged it to Mom's credit card I had for emergencies because F her. I wasn't ready to be alone so I sat in the reception room completely terrified about how I'd explain everything to Mel. The lounge was filled with guests having drinks before dinner and everyone looked content and relaxed in the plush surroundings that served as their home away from home. I had never felt more out of place in my life because I no longer had a home. Going back to live with Mom and Alicia was out of the question. Even returning to Boulder felt like a stretch. I had ten grand to live off of but my entire life fit into one small backpack, which made me feel pretty inconsequential. There were people riding the gondola that afternoon who had brought along bigger, fuller bags just for the ride.

A waitress from the bar brought over a bowl of snack mix along with a napkin and asked if I wanted a drink and then suggested, "Like a Shirley Temple or an iced tea?"

I was so grateful she saw me as a minor I could have hugged her. "What I'd really like is a home-cooked meal," I replied.

"Then you should try Little Annie's," she said. "They have a dish called Grandma's Mac-N-Cheese that's right up your alley."

I smiled and said, "I'm actually more interested in the home than the meal."

She laughed and replied, "This is Aspen. You've come to the wrong town for that."

"What's the right town?"

"The one with the most people you love," she said, and crossed the room to serve someone else.

For hours I sat in the lounge and watched hotel guests drift away in pairs and small groups to enjoy if not their lives then at least their plans for the night. When I was the last person remaining and there was no one left to stare at except my reflection in the glass fireplace doors I conceded my life was in ruins. The hardest thing to accept was that if I had just told Mom everything two years earlier the outcome, though not pretty, would still have been better.

The same was true for Melanie. I should have told her about Alicia sooner but I knew my confession would also be our last goodbye and I was so afraid to lose her. Our biology textbook said it was impossible for the human brain to feel both gratitude and fear simultaneously so I stayed in the lounge and considered all my reasons to feel grateful. I started with the good times Mom and I managed to share. There were some and it wasn't all bad and my fear subsided as I sat there feeling lucky for myself. I thought of even more reasons to be grateful. The ones I liked best involved Melanie—our golf games together, sharing her iPod at school, hanging out in her bedroom and watching her organizing her shelves. The girl always had me spellbound. Everything about her was staggering; even the way she folded her laundry.

Once my fears subsided I went upstairs and sat on the floor outside Mel's room and used my backpack as a cushion against her door. A little bit later Mel arrived. When she saw me sitting at her door she immediately stopped and yelled down the hallway, "I asked you to walk the other way if you saw me, not stalk me!" Mel was always such a hard-ass; it was one of the reasons I loved her.

I hopped to my feet and threw my pack over my shoulder. Mel wasn't gonna come one step closer and she was all the way down the hallway. I was afraid she'd turn around and leave and I had to tell her the truth so I shouted, "I had sex with my godmother when I was fifteen years old and if you don't mind I'd kinda like to talk to you about it!"

Mel sprinted to the door and pushed me inside the room with her. "What is the matter with you?"

"I had to get it off my chest Mel. I'm in love with you and I know I ruined everything already but I had to tell you anyway."

Mel shut her door. "Are you talking about Alicia?" I nodded and her nose crinkled with revulsion. "When you were fifteen?" I nodded again. She thought a bit and said, "That's really messed up. I'm sorry."

jimmy gleacher

It rained reasons to love her—for her compassion, for her insight, for her composure. I felt blessed just to know her but it was bittersweet knowing she'd never feel the same way about me.

"Thank you," I said. "It pretty much went on the entire year we lived here in Aspen and then it stopped, but then it started again a few months ago."

Mel lifted her chin and stared down her nose at me with a penetrating look that said she understood what I was saying. She digested the news calmly—another reason to love her—but she kept her mouth shut and let me twist in the wind. The girl knew how to fight and I loved her for that too.

"I'm sorry Mel. I didn't know how to stop it. I tried to avoid her. I'd sleep at Harmony's Rest and stay in the library until it closed. I ate dinners at Lucky's and even bought a lock for my bedroom door, but on some level I must have wanted it too, which is the hardest thing to explain."

Mel thought overtime to try and make sense of the situation to help us both understand, when she had every reason in the world to tell me I was worthless and throw me out the door and I loved her for that.

"It didn't even make me feel good," I said.

"Then why'd you keep doing it?"

"It was a tragic expression of an unmet need."

"Needs I couldn't meet and yet there I was throwing myself at you like an idiot."

"It wasn't about sex, Mel. It was about having no father and a mother who'd be smiling one minute and throwing china against the wall the next minute. It was about wanting someone to tuck me into bed even if it meant them sleeping with me. And when I was older it was simply about hating myself and perpetuating a cycle so I could feel that way."

Mel's arms were still crossed. My little speech did nothing to soften her. She was tough as nails and I loved her for that. Then she smirked and said, *A tragic expression of an unmet need*? You've been thinking about this a lot, haven't you?" She smiled just enough to lighten the mood a little bit and boy did I love her for that.

"I came up with it in the lounge about an hour ago," I replied.

"It's nice. But you really shouldn't hate yourself. You're the most responsible kid in our school."

"It was all a big lie. You said it yourself. I should have told you sooner."

"You tried," she said, "but I stopped you because I wanted the perfect boyfriend and I'm sorry for making you carry that secret even longer."

"You did nothing wrong," I said.

"I didn't make you feel safe."

"I think you're really pretty Mel. The only reason I didn't sleep with you is because I couldn't until you knew the truth."

"And now I know."

"Actually, there's something else. Your parents."

"Mom told me. Ketamine. She also promised nothing happened with you two and I believe her."

"Do you believe me?" I asked.

"I do. I'm sorry I even doubted you but it looked pretty bad when Mindy found your caddy bib after you swore you weren't in the den with them."

"Mel, I would never ever touch your mother. I know it sounds crazy after everything I just told you but I really do love you way too much to do something like that."

Mel smiled. "That doesn't sound crazy at all. It actually sounds kinda nice."

The girl was a gift.

"So, did you and your mom talk about why I drugged them?" I asked her.

"Mom said kids will be kids."

"Are you happy with that?"

"What's the alternative?"

"The truth."

"That my dad is gay and so ashamed to admit it he has to be drunk all the time which only makes things worse because then he can't control himself and feels my boyfriend's ass right in front of me? Yeah, I think I'll stick with 'Kids will be kids.'"

We sat next to each other on the edge of her bed, two kids alone in a hotel. Mel folded her hands in her lap and said, "I'm sorry about my parents. And I'm sorry about your parents too."

"Grown-ups will be grown-ups," I said.

This made her smile and I loved her smile. She looked at me with playful suspicion and asked, "What did you say to my mom this afternoon? I've never seen her in such a good mood."

And though I had learned the valuable lesson that honesty is always the best policy I had also learned that a well-placed omission is sometimes even better and telling Mel about her mom and Timmy Timmy Timmy would be worse than telling her the truth. "I told her how much I loved you. I told her she should get a divorce. And I told her if she wanted to have fun then she should have a little fun."

Mel furrowed her brow. "You told my mom to have an affair? How did you even get on the topic?"

"We had a Come to Jesus, Mel. I laid it all on the line because I'm totally freaked out they're gonna have me arrested."

"Well you should be," Mel said, and I loved how she could be so unsparing. "They were pretty upset this morning but then again they both seemed pretty damn happy tonight, so who knows?" Mel grabbed my hand and stood up. She walked me to the door and said, "Good luck with your match tomorrow."

"It's against my dad," I said.

Her eyes popped and she laughed and replied, "Well then you better kick his ass something fierce." She didn't want to know any more information like who he was or how we found each other or what the match was for. She'd moved around enough earth for one day and wanted to kick back and watch a movie in bed. Kids will be kids, and that's exactly what Mel was and that's exactly what Mel wanted to be. And that was the biggest reason of all to love her: the girl knew herself well and had no regrets about who she was.

Mel opened the door and said, "Good luck out there." She pointed her fingers at me like a gun and winked and she looked so goddamned cute doing it I swear I could have gone and hung myself.

the blink of an eye

i woke up the next morning in the hotel's luxurious bed and stared at my immaculate surroundings. Everything from the bedside table's reading lamp to the hotel's pen and pad of paper had an established setting and each item was in its proper spot. I occupied a sliver of the fluffed bedding and my ratty backpack rested on a leather chair that faced a curtained window. Me and my meager belongings didn't have a place in the room or anywhere else in the world and it was time to go out and find one.

After a long shower and a big breakfast ordered up from room service (thanks Mom!) I rode the bus to Ed's golf club and walked down the impressively long cobblestone entrance lined with aspen trees and magnolias. Within minutes a guy appeared in a golf cart. He was my age and probably worked the bag drop just like I did at the BGC. I told him I was a guest of a member named Ed and he asked, "Ed who?" Then he blinked both his eyes as if he had a sharp sinus pain.

"I don't know his last name."

"Where're your clubs?" He blinked again.

"They're coming," I said. He was right to be suspicious; I must have looked like a vagrant wandering aimlessly in my cheap clothes and toting a tattered backpack.

He smirked like he didn't believe me and replied, "Sorry, but I can't let you in here without a member."

"I understand," I said, "but I'm playing Ed for a lot of money and I've never seen the course so I was hoping to get a quick look. I was supposed to play here yesterday but didn't make it."

He laughed. "Ah, you must be playing with Mr. Ellis." His eyes shut for a split second, then he continued to regard me as suspect. "How do you and Mr. Ellis know each other?"

"We don't but I'm pretty sure he's my father."

That really cracked him up and he didn't blink. "You do kinda look like him and with Mr. Ellis anything's possible! He mentioned something about a few guests yesterday but nothing about one of them being his son."

"He was here yesterday?"

Blink, blink. "Spent the whole afternoon in the shed."

"The shed?"

"That's what we call our indoor teaching facility. It's got the top-of-the-line video analysis to measure swing angles, ball speed, launch angles, you name it. We got digital putting analysis, hitting nets, a putting green, a chipping area, a sand trap and a course simulator. Mr. Ellis spent the entire day in there all alone. He must've had about five hours of lessons and I heard he played thirty-six at St. Andrews and eighteen at Pebble Beach on the simulator."

"Guess he was getting ready for our match," I said.

"Oh, he was grinding big-time." He smiled, then blinked.

"So can I check out the course?"

"No but get in the cart and I'll give you a ride back out to the road."

I sat next to him and said, "I'm Gates." We shook hands.

"I'm Mike but everyone around here calls me Rain Man."

"Because of the whole blinking thing? Don't worry about it. I caddy in Boulder and my nickname there is Fun Buns."

He laughed and said, "Nicknames are a bitch, aren't they? We got a caddy here named Pat, but he dresses like he's in a boy band so everyone calls him Smooth Pat." He chuckled. "Pat can't stand it. Fights it tooth and nail, but that just makes it stick even harder. Even the members call him Smooth Pat." He laughed again.

"But you don't mind Rain Man?" I asked.

He shook his head and said, "It's the damnedest thing. I don't blink when I'm playing golf or skiing or doing pretty much anything I like but as soon as I have to be still for even a millisecond it's like my eyes take over."

"Sounds like a psych issue to me," I said. "Bet you could fix it."

He blinked. "Yeah, Mr. Ellis has actually been paying for me to see a shrink in town, been a big help."

I felt the oddest ping of envy that Ed had taken an interest in this guy who wasn't even his son. Then I felt ridiculous.

Rain Man dropped me off back at the road and said, "See ya in there, Fun Buns," which I had to admit was pretty funny.

There was nowhere to sit by the entrance so it wasn't exactly a great place to chill. I called Timmy Timmy Timmy to see if he had made contact with Mrs. Vanleer but got his voicemail so he must have been hard at work either smiling or pouting, or as he liked to put it—smouting. 3T's hated being a model. His parents got him into it when he was five and he swears that's when he developed his OCD. When he'd get discouraged he'd pull out his portfolio and flip through the pictures from various jobs and chant, "Car car car. Mortgage mortgage mortgage. College college college," like a mantra to calm him. His parents were good people. They put their house in his name, set him up as an LLC and treated his modeling as nothing more than a very fortunate financial opportunity. They made it very clear he could quit at any time, which is probably why he stuck with it for so long.

Ed's car arrived a few minutes later. Piper drove and Ed rode shotgun. Lu was in the back and he popped open the door and scowled at me. I hopped in and said, "Nice of you to show up Mr. Ellis," in a nasty tone to let Ed know he blew any chance of winning me over by not stopping at Alicia's.

The bag drop at Ed's club had large potted plants, fancy wooden benches and a large bronzed statue of a big-horned elk where the cars pulled up. At the BGC we had an orange traffic cone Lu stole from the city and a sandwich board from a bankrupt deli Lu spray-painted white and stenciled with black letters: BAG DROP. The silhouette of the defunct deli's mascot, a waving pickle wearing a sombrero, could still be seen beneath the spray paint. Ed jumped out of the car and loudly announced, "I've got a special guest today Rain Man." He slapped my back and grabbed the nape of my neck. "This here is the Colorado junior golf champion for the past three years in a row. Throw his clubs on the back of one cart and mine on another and pull up a third for his buddy here." Ed motioned toward Lu but Rain Man was already transfixed by his outfit. Lu was wearing yellow knickers tucked into powder blue socks stretched up to his knees. The socks matched his tie, which was secured to his white oxford shirt with a silver clip. On his head was a white straw panama hat with a yellow band to complement his pants. Lu fingered a leaf on one of the plants to check if it was real. He looked Rain Man up and down and in his Confucius voice said, "Man who read woman like book prefer braille." Rain Man didn't blink.

Ed and I went to the range and when he set up next to me I took my bag and walked as far away from him as possible. Lu stood a few feet behind me with his arms crossed and watched me hit as if he were some kind of swing coach. I kept catching glimpses of his yellow knickers and powder blue socks. After a couple of swings I turned around and said, "Don't stand there and watch me practice as if you're on my side."

He looked at me like I was crazy and asked, "Who wants you to win more than me?"

"Then drop the threat of having me arrested."

Without confirmation from Timmy Timmy Timmy that he'd successfully completed his cougar-capturing photo mission of Mrs. Vanleer I couldn't be sure I was safe from the police. After our conversation in her hotel room she was definitely spooked by my threat to push old Marty out of the closet if they involved the cops but she was a loose cannon and if she was planning on divorcing him she might even want me to tell the world his secret. The only way I could feel entirely secure was if 3T's smouted his way into her heart and got some scandalous pictures in return. Mrs. Vanleer wouldn't press charges if my best friend had photos of her naked; she'd be too afraid I'd retaliate and post them all over the BGC. I loved Mel way too much to humiliate her mom, but I would have felt a lot better knowing I had them as bargaining chips.

"Just win and it won't matter," Lu said. "Besides, it's not so much a threat as it is a motivation."

"Well it's not exactly inspiring me."

"It will."

"For once just do something good for someone else Lu. That would inspire me."

Lu lifted his panama hat and like Confucius said, "You want peace on earth? Man who lay woman on ground get piece on earth."

"Go stand somewhere else," I barked. "You look like a tranny elf and I can't concentrate with you around."

I moved through my irons, hybrids, woods and hit everything pure. At the practice green I blasted a few bunker shots, hit a few chips and got familiar with the putting surface. The greens rolled true and were the only straightforward thing in my life. The course was my ally. Gravity and physics were its sole manipulations; it wasn't motivated by money, lust, a midlife crisis or guilt. My swing was as free and easy as it had ever been and Ed didn't stand a chance. I looked down the range and caught him staring at me. His face was filled with pride for his son's ability, my ability, and it made me wish he'd seen me win those three state tourneys. I wanted to tell him my GPA was a 4.0. Then I realized it didn't matter how good my swing was that morning: he still had the advantage.

Just before we were about to tee off Rain Man brought me his personal yardage book. On each page he had written meticulous notes about where to aim off the tee, yardages to ideal landing zones, which way the greens break, where to miss. Some of the writing was smudged with dirt and sweat and on the bottom of every page he had written himself messages like *Cooking pumpkin seeds on Halloween* and *Brand-new socks*. These were his good memories and things he liked. They kept him from blinking. "Some of them are kinda corny," he said sheepishly.

I laughed. "Thanks. I don't know why you're being so nice to me, but thanks."

"Mr. Ellis brings a lot of guests here," he explained. "You're the first one who showed up on foot carrying a backpack."

"Who's he usually bring?"

Rain Man blinked. "Oh, he keeps it pretty entertaining around here."

"So all the guys like him?" A member's rep in the caddy shack is the best way to gauge his true character.

"No . . . they worship him. He's not perfect, but he doesn't pretend to be either." We looked down the range at Ed and this time it was me filled with pride.

Ed, Lu and I met on the first tee and agreed to play an eighteen-hole match play closeout, meaning the contest was scored hole by hole, not stroke by stroke. The pot was a hundred grand, Lu's fifty versus Ed's. Lu left the tee box and we looked down the first fairway in silence. Very casually I said, "You want a little side action?"

The question humored Ed. "I didn't realize I was playing with the Cincinnati Kid. What kind of action?"

"Ten grand a hole?" I showed him the bank-issued 10K brick from my backpack.

Ed grinned and asked, "What about the other seventeen holes?"

"Don't worry, I'll have twice as much on the next tee."

That really tickled him and he gestured for me to hit, which was his way of consenting to the bet. Rain Man's yardage book recommended hitting a three-wood at the right fairway bunker. At the bottom of the page he had written, *Pizza in December*.

Ed saw me grab my three-wood and said, "Someone's

done their homework. I thought you and Piper sat on top of the mountain and gabbed all day."

"We did. That's a fine ambassador you have there Mr. Ellis. Rain Man lent me his yardage book."

Ed raised his eyebrows. "Ah, the Holy Grail."

All the coolness I'd had on the range was gone. My hand shook so much I had a tough time balancing the ball on the tee. *Pizza in December,* I thought to myself and it actually calmed me down enough make a decent swing and get my shot in the fairway.

Ed spoke as he teed up his ball with a driver in his hand: "Rain Man's a solid caddy but he's also a pussy." He blasted his shot over the treetops lining the left side of the fairway. We hopped in our carts and headed down the hole. Ed's shot had successfully cut the corner of the dogleg and was sixty yards ahead of mine. As I selected a club he said, "The ball flies farther up here," in a genuine attempt to be helpful. My second shot missed the green but got a lucky bounce off a mound in the rough onto the putting surface and slowly trickled to ten feet from the hole. Ed said, "That's what we call an O. J. Simpson: you got away with it," and drove down the fairway.

I jumped in my cart and followed him. He read the yardage off a sprinkler head and grabbed a wedge. His movements were swift and confident and just as he was about to step into his stance I asked, "So how was Houston?"

He took half a step back and looked at me curiously. "Houston was Houston. Ever been?"

"No, but I hear it looks just like an indoor golf facility."

Ed skulled his simple chip shot off the back of the green and into some tall fescue and that was how I won the first hole and more importantly seized the psychological advantage by letting Ed know I knew he was full of crap.

Even so, he was all smiles on the next tee and cheerfully asked, "Double or nothing?"

The hole was a 440-yard par 4 that played straight uphill and was bisected by a creek 240 yards from the tee where any good drive would land. Rain Man's book said not to be suckered into trying to clear the creek so I laid up with a five-wood. Ed hit his drive into the water and I won that hole too. So I was two up for Lu and up thirty G's from Ed. On the next tee he said, "Well Cincinnati, that's gotta be the easiest thirty thousand dollars you've ever made in your life."

"Do you really think this is easy for me Mr. Ellis?"

"Call me Ed."

"I'd rather stick to formalities."

"Okay. How much you wanna play this one for, *Mr.* Cincinnati?"

"How 'bout all thirty?"

He shook his head. "The match is young. Put some of your winnings aside; it's a tough hole, especially if you've never played it before."

"That's very big of you Mr. Ellis," I said. "Let's play for ten then."

The third hole was a short par 3 with a severe elevation drop that made the mileage hard to gauge. Rain Man's book said to club down and the note he'd written was *Ally Dexter's ass, sophomore year*, which made me wonder what it looked like her junior year. My shot came up short and buried in a bunker. Ed silently went about his business and landed his ball on the green, which he two-putted for the win.

We played the fourth hole for ten thousand and he won that too, which evened up the match with Lu and brought Ed's tab down to ten G's. All my confidence from the range had vanished and my swing was MIA. Fortunately Ed wasn't playing well either. He was wild off the tee but managed to find the green one way or the other. He hit his best shots and was most comfortable whenever he was on the brink of disaster, which explained a lot about his personality.

We tied holes five through eleven and there was very little chatter. I was curious about Ed's reasons for trying to reconnect but content to just play golf and wait him out because he wasn't being straight with me. He made a few attempts at small talk but my answers were monosyllabic and I knew the longer he waited to come out with the truth the better the chances were he'd just spit it out. I was slowly discovering this was my father's style, and in that manner we were very much alike.

When we reached the twelfth hole we caught up to a foursome, the only other group on the course. They were barely off the tee and were walking so we had a good wait until we could hit. Ed said, "I know this guy," referring to the member in the group ahead of us. "He ain't gonna let us play through."

"Why not?" I asked.

He shook his head. "I kinda used to date his wife."

"Were they still married?"

"It's not that simple."

"It's never simple with you is it Mr. Ellis?"

Ed thought this over. After a bit he said, "Your mom's a tough case."

I nodded and replied, "Her girlfriend's even tougher."

The group in front of us cleared and Ed looked confused as he teed up his ball. He made a tired swing like his heart was heavy and his shot sailed way right and out of bounds. Number twelve was an easy hole. Rain Man's book suggested a five-iron off the tee. The note at the bottom said *Sunday morning.* The small exchange with Ed and the break in the action calmed my nerves, and my swing from the range returned. Ed whistled at how purely I struck the ball and said, "Thatta boy," with genuine encouragement even though he knew he'd lose the hole. He really was hard not to like.

So I was back to one up for Lu and up twenty G's from

Ed. We agreed to play number thirteen for ten and if I could win that one I'd be set for boarding school. The hole was wide open and played downhill into a valley. The green was surrounded by a bowl of earth. A good drive could get home and Rain Man's book actually suggested going for it. At the bottom of the page he had drawn a Nike swoosh. I smoked my drive all the way down the hill to the middle of the green. It wasn't hard; gravity did most of the work.

Ed was about to hit but then he asked me, "What did you mean about Alicia?"

"Oh, so you knew about her?"

"Of course I knew about her."

"But you didn't know about me?"

His shoulders slumped. "I didn't." He made another tired swing that hooked into the valley wall but got a good bounce and rolled all the way down the fairway to the front of the green. I was happy for his good fortune. Playing golf makes one very karmically aware. Playfully I asked, "Whattaya call that? An O. J. Simpson?" to try and make him feel better.

He shook his head in disgust and said, "Every once in a while even a blind squirrel finds a nut."

In Lu's Confucius voice I said, "Squirrel who climb lady's leg not find nuts." I didn't know where the urge to crack a joke came from. I wanted to be pissed at Ed and

win as much of his money as possible but there I was rooting for him and trying to cheer him up. Ed didn't laugh so
I explained, "Sorry, Lu's always making jokes like that."

We stood at our carts by the tee. Lu was halfway down
the fairway. His blue and yellow outfit made him stick out
like a campy smurf. Ed asked, "What's the deal with that
guy anyway?"

"You mean the guy you're gambling with so you can
anonymously meet your long-lost son? What kind of a guy
do you think he is Mr. Ellis? Here's a hint: the only reason
I'm here right now is because he threatened to have me arrested if I didn't come and win." I hopped in my cart and
drove away. My emotions were swinging more than my
golf clubs and with way less control. Ed was so distracted
he yanked his shot over the green into a small patch of
pine trees and conceded the hole without even looking for
his ball, so I went two up for Lu, and up thirty G's in the
side bet.

Number thirteen was a par 3 and we caught up to the
group ahead of us again and were forced to wait. Ed paced
on the tee. He was agitated and shot angry glances at Lu.
"What's he threatening to turn you into the cops for?" he
asked me.

Real wise-assy I replied, "Mmm, that's probably something I should only discuss with my parents Mr. Ellis."

Ed bounced the ball on the face of his iron. He was

thinking real hard and I couldn't wait to hear his response. Then I realized just how much fun I was actually having but it kinda felt like a punch in the stomach because there was still so much of me that wanted to begrudge this man. He was less reliable than the mountain weather and I didn't want to let myself enjoy his company because I might never be in it again. Ed clenched his ball in his palm and said, "How 'bout if I win you tell me what Lu could get you arrested for?"

"Fine. And if I win you tell me one thing that isn't a lie."

The hole was only 130 yards but the landing area was surrounded by water. The yardage book said ignore the pin and aim for the middle of the green. For inspiration Rain Man had scribbled *Powder . . .* , which was fitting for a dude from Aspen but I had never skied in my life and got to thinking how I was one of the few kids from Boulder who'd never even been on a chairlift. This made me feel even more separated from my peers, along with the bizarre game of golf truth-or-dare I was playing with my estranged father. I wondered if I was destined to be an outcast for my entire life, and was this as good as it was ever gonna get? All this was racing through my head as I made my swing and I shanked it into the water. That's golf and I couldn't wait to tee it up once more and try again.

Ed smoothed a beautiful wedge high into the air that never left the pin and came straight down fifteen feet from the cup. I conceded the hole after missing my putt for bogey and said, "I drugged my girlfriend's parents," as I picked up his ball mark and tossed it to him.

"What the hell you do that for?"

I shook my head and said, "Gonna have to win another hole to find that out, Mr. Ellis."

"You're on, and just to pay it forward here's something true: I'm a coward." He looked me right in the eyes. "Five days ago you played some men from Omaha who happen to be longtime business pals of mine and one of them called me and said he met a kid in Boulder who had my old putter." He took the custom-made Scotty Cameron from my bag. "There's only two of these in the world."

"I remember that guy," I said. "He tried to buy it off me."

"He did!" Ed just thought that was the funniest thing in the word. "How much?"

"Five hundred bucks." I started to laugh too even though I had no idea what was so funny.

Ed slapped his knee and asked, "Why the hell didn't you take the money and run?"

The question rendered me silent and then that stillness spread across the golf course through Lu and the foursome in front of us and not even Rain Man was blinking. A squirrel's tail hitting the ground would've sounded like thunder. "I don't know," I said. "I guess maybe I knew it was yours."

Ed grabbed the back of my neck and shook me gently.

He hung his head with shame and said, "I should have called your mother right then and demanded an explanation but instead I went through this whole ridiculous charade and I'm sorry."

"So why'd you give Mom the putter?"

"I didn't. She must've stolen it out of my bag before I left." We both fell silent and tried to unravel the mysteries of Mom. Then Ed said, "Every storm has an eye. Maybe in a brief moment of calmness she wanted a piece of me to give to you. She's not all bad, but she's a helluva twister."

"So where's the other putter?" I asked, because Ed putted with a Ping Anser 2 and not a Scotty Cameron like mine.

"Dubai," he said. "I lost it to a Saudi so wealthy he only liked to play for his opponent's most personal possessions."

"What did he put up?"

"I'd rather not say."

I shook my head and said, "I used to think about what it'd be like if I ever met my father and this isn't even close." We shared a good laugh at that one. We had already finished thirteen out of eighteen holes and were finally just beginning to connect but after seventeen years it felt like the blink of an eye.

the nineteenth hole

i could have won the fourteenth hole but missed an easy putt on purpose so I could tell Ed about Marty, my nickname and how I snapped. The group ahead of us took their time looking for a ball in the rough. They were playing extra slowly to piss off Ed but their plan backfired because we were in no rush. Ed lackadaisically swung his driver with one arm to stay loose. He looked around and took in the beauty of our surroundings. He was very much at home and at peace with himself. His contentment was contagious because even I began to relax.

"Here's another truth," he said earnestly. "You could resent me for the rest of your life and I wouldn't blame you. And yes, I wasn't in Houston yesterday. I was too chicken to pick you up at the airport and too chicken to stop at Alicia's house."

"But you're the one who sought me out so why go through all the trouble to meet me and then hide?"

"I didn't even know you existed until a few days ago and then all of a sudden I might be your father and it scared the shit out of me."

"You don't need to worry. I don't want anything from you."

He shook his head. "It's not about that. It's about who I am, who I understand myself to be. After we walk off the eighteenth green you may never talk to me again and I'm prepared to accept that but just knowing you're out there feels like the greatest opportunity in my life."

"Thanks, Ed," I said. He smiled because I didn't call him Mr. Ellis. The group ahead of us cleared. "I'm up thirty grand. Wanna chance to win some of your money back?" I asked him.

"I think I should stop while I'm behind."

"I don't want to play for truths anymore," I said.

Ed pensively tapped a spot on the ground with the toe of his driver. He had hoped for a better response to his speech. "We got four holes left," he said. "Let's just play golf."

"You sure? I thought you needed something on the line to make it interesting."

He smiled. "This is plenty interesting. Besides, we're all square in the middle of a pretty big bet, remember?" He pointed his club down the fairway at Lu.

"Oh yeah. I almost forgot."

"You almost forgot about possibly going to jail?" He raised his eyebrows. "Because I was gonna lose on purpose just to keep you out of the clink."

"Really?" I asked him. "You'd do that for me?"

Ed replied, "What do you think?" as if the answer should have been obvious.

"Lu can't get me arrested. I already smoothed things out with the Vanleers but he doesn't know." This wasn't exactly true but I wanted Ed to believe I was in the clear so he could keep his fifty grand and even more importantly think I had my life under control.

"And you still showed up to play?"

"I had my reasons," I said. "But just so you know, we're all square too. In life that is." That was my reason for being there, to forgive Ed and move on. It was easier than I thought and felt even better. If I knew where Gervaise lived I'd write her a thank-you note.

"So what do you want to do about this match for Lu?" Ed asked.

"How 'bout I let you win and we split the money? Lu was gonna have me arrested and he's a thief too," I said to build my case for essentially stealing Lu's money. "And he's a compulsive gambler so anything he wins is just gonna end up with a bookie."

Ed mulled over my words. "What would you do with all that cash?"

"Boarding school next year, then college."

"You really want to spend your senior year at a boarding school? What about all your friends? Your girlfriend?"

"Anywhere is better than home."

Very carefully Ed replied, "Piper mentioned you hinted about a few things concerning Alicia . . ."

"How'd you know she and Mom were girlfriends?" I asked to change the subject.

"I met her a few times and could tell something was going on between them, but your mom was pretty good at keeping a secret. Who knows that better than us, right?" He smiled and it made me want to talk more.

"Why'd you leave her?" I asked.

"We weren't a good match."

"That's not a good enough answer."

"It's complicated."

"You can tell me what happened," I said.

"No," he answered. "I can't." Ed was too good a man to trash Mom by telling me the truth. After a moment of silence he said, "If Alicia was inappropriate with you say the word and I'll go after her."

I looked him in the eye and replied, "Thanks."

Ed nodded and cleared all the heavy air gathered around us by jovially saying, "Hey, remember my friend Paula from the other day? She knew you were my son the second she met you and I didn't even tell her. Halfway through the second hole she said to me, 'Holy shit Ed, I think that's your kid. How many others do you have spread around the globe?'"

"I remember you guys laughing," I told him. "I guess that's why she called me Oliver Twist on the next tee."

Ed chuckled but then very seriously told me, "You're the only one, Gates. I want you to know that."

"Mr. Ellis," I said, "I'm very glad we met." I wasn't about to open up about Alicia and my crazy life with Mom. He'd have to earn that and it would take a lot more than a round of golf but the best thing about Ed was he understood.

We made a pact to throw the match and had a blast putting on a heartbreaking show for Lu. Ed three-putted the fifteenth hole so I could go one up. Then on sixteen we both made good pars. On seventeen, a par 5, Ed reached the green with a spectacular second shot and made a tap-in birdie to tie the match. On the eighteenth tee he said, "This is more fun than the real thing."

"Just make sure you hit your drive in the fairway," I told him. "If you hit it OB it's gonna look pretty suspicious if I do the same."

Ed teed up his ball and as he stood over it he looked up at me and said, "This is the most nervous I've been about a golf shot in my entire life."

I pulled out Rain Man's yardage book. On the bottom of the sheet for eighteen he had written *Home*. I told Ed this and he flexed his knees and piped a beauty right down the middle.

The kind thing for me to do would have been to shank my drive and put Lu out of his misery but I kept his hopes alive all the way to the final six-foot putt I needed to sink in order to tie the match. The putt had four inches of break, I allowed for three and that one inch of earth separating my ball from the bottom of the cup was as full of possibilities as a vast, undiscovered land.

Lu took the loss like a man. Right on the green he gave Ed five stacks of a hundred hundred-dollar bills kept in place with a $10,000 bank ribbon. He shook Ed's hand and said, "Maybe next time."

Ed replied, "There won't be a next time."

"I didn't think so," Lu said.

Ed walked to his cart and put his gear away. I hung my head and said, "Sorry Lu. I choked."

Stoically Lu replied, "He hit a great shot on seventeen. What can you do?"

I waited for a threat or a Confucius joke or something but Lu had nothing else to say. I held up Rain Man's booklet and told him, "I gotta go find that caddy and give him back his yardage book, so I'll meet you in the parking lot."

Lu drove his cart toward the front of the club and Ed and I went in the other direction. We found Rain Man and a caddy with elaborately sculpted sideburns and a goatee engaged in a heated competition of chipping wedge shots through a tire hanging from a branch behind the caddy shack. When Ed saw them he shouted, "I want action!" He pointed at the caddy bedazzled with facial hair and said, "Smooth Pat, let me borrow your wedge," and Rain Man looked at me and grinned.

Both guys shook their heads and Rain Man said, "I've lost enough money today as it is, Mr. Ellis." He looked at me and asked, "So how'd it go out there?"

I handed him his yardage book and replied, "It was perfect and your book made it even better, so thanks."

"Who won?" Rain Man asked. He didn't blink with Ed around.

"We tied," I said.

"No sudden death? No playoff?" He looked at Ed for an explanation.

"A tie's good," Ed said.

I grabbed my backpack from the cart and we headed into the men's locker room through a heavy wooden unmarked door. Ed led me through a lounge where some men played dice at a round table. They greeted Ed like he was the governor. We passed into a much larger room with couches and leather padded benches in front of large wooden lockers. Each one had a member's last name engraved on a brass plate that was drilled onto the door. At the far side of the room was an old wooden bar tended by an old wooden man in a black tie and jacket.

We sat on a bench in front of the ELLIS locker and Ed took out his checkbook and wrote me a note for thirty thousand dollars and said, "If you need more for school let me know."

"I think I'll be covered," I said. "To be honest I don't really feel right taking this."

"A bet's a bet and you won fair and square." He handed me the five bricks of cash Lu had given him and said, "But you gotta give this back to Lu. That was fun putting on a show but we can't take this guy's money."

"He's just gonna lose it," I said.

"That's not your problem. But if you keep his money, down the road you'll regret it and then it will be your problem."

I stuffed Lu's cash in my backpack and tried not to think of it as my college tuition. Ed was giving me good advice, fatherly advice, and the experience was worth more than money.

Ed wrote his cell phone number on the back of his business card and handed it to me. "I'm sorry things have been so bad at home. You can stay with me anytime and there's a pretty good boarding school twenty miles down the road in Carbondale that I know for sure I can get you into so you could go there and stay with me on the holidays."

A sparkle in his eye made me ask, "How are you so sure you can get me in?"

His gaze darted around the room quickly and he replied, "The chairman of the board of trustees owes me a favor . . . don't ask."

I laughed and said, "Thanks for the golf. And thanks for the advice too."

Ed slipped into a simple pair of sneakers and hopped up and said, "Come on, my ambassador gets angry if I keep her waiting."

Piper had the car pulled up out front. Lu was in the backseat staring out the open window like a Labrador. Our bags had been driven around and loaded and just as I was climbing into the car Rain Man ran up to me and handed me his yardage book. He blinked really hard and said, "A souvenir."

I was genuinely touched and asked, "Really?"

He nodded and blinked hard again and said, "Check out the nineteenth hole."

I flipped to the last page of the booklet as we drove away from the club. Rain Man had written: 19th HOLE.

Par: Infinity. And his positive swing thought was *Playing golf with Dad*.

It was a short drive to the airport and no one said a word. The silence was unbearable so I took the CD with the six cello suites from my backpack and passed it forward to Ed. He liked the music and I let him keep it. The plane was ready and waiting and we were driven right out onto the tarmac to the little flight of stairs dangling from the jet's open door. Piper and Ed drove away as soon as my clubs were loaded and we climbed aboard. There were no big goodbyes. Everything that needed to be said had been said. All that was left was the future and for that we'd have to wait and see.

The stewardess lifted up the hatch door and locked us in for our flight. Lu immediately went to the bathroom and changed into madras shorts and a kelly green polo shirt. He sat across from me and I asked, "You gonna have me arrested now?"

He shook his head.

"You said you would."

"I thought it'd be easy money."

"You turned on me pretty bad Lu. Wade too. We're just dumb kids. We might act all tough and grown-up but we're not."

"There's something wrong with me but all I can do is try and fix it." He thought a moment. "The first thing I need to do is win some money. Get back on my feet."

"Brilliant," I said.

"If you got a better idea I'm all ears."

"Stop gambling. Save your money. Pay your mortgage."

He laughed. "Gates, I've won and lost way more than fifty thousand dollars on one bet before. I'll be fine. Besides, thirty-six of that fifty I just won a few days ago so I really only lost fourteen, ten of which you could have lost the first time you played Ed so we're really only down four grand if you look at it that way." That's what's called gambler's logic, Lu's version of Paradise Rules.

"There is no more *we,* Lu. I'm done."

The stewardess walked down the aisle to make sure our seat belts were buckled and the pilot announced into a soft intercom that we'd be taking off shortly.

"Will you at least still caddy?" Lu asked. "I promise not to send you out with Marty again."

"I don't know what I'm gonna do," I said.

"The course will always be available to you."

"Thanks."

"I'm sorry about everything. It's a sickness. What can I say?"

"You seem relieved," I told him.

He nodded and replied, "When you spend all your waking hours waiting for the bottom to fall out it's always a relief when it finally happens."

The plane shot forward and within seconds we were

soaring. When we got to Boulder I asked Lu to stop by our bank. I told him I had to make a withdrawal and ran in to deposit Ed's check and my brick of cash. It was Saturday but fortunately Lu's mortgage broker Paul was there. I pointed out the window where Lu was waiting in the car and told him, "Lu sent me in to make a deposit for the club's payments."

Paul furrowed his brow and asked, "Why isn't he coming in?"

"I think he's embarrassed."

"I didn't think it was possible for Lu to feel embarrassed," he replied. "You've seen how he dresses right?"

"I think Lu's embarrassed all the time. That's why he does the things he does and says the things he says." I handed over all fifty thousand dollars. "Better deposit this before he changes his mind."

Paul shook his head in disbelief and looked back and forth between the money in his hands and Lu. He muttered, "It belongs to the bank now," and walked away.

Even though I stole Lu's fortune I used it to pay off his debt so hopefully hell can wait another day for me. When I got back in Lu's car I didn't tell him. Instead I let him bask in the glory of his self-fulfilled prophecy of failure a little longer. Everyone has their comfort zones.

We remained silent for the rest of the drive to the BGC and when we pulled into the lot our club seemed so much less grand than Ed's but it felt like home. Lu parked the car and shut the engine but didn't move to open his door. He turned to me and said, "I don't want you to beat yourself up about losing my money. You tried your best and you played well and I want you to be proud. We can't win 'em all so don't let this discourage you, okay?"

As embarrassing as it is to admit, Lu's words made my eyes get all hot and wet and it took all my restraint to keep it together. It had been an emotional day, week, two years, but all that was behind me. I managed to fake a smile and replied, "Thanks, Lu."

In his regular voice Lu said, "Just remember, Confucius says our greatest glory is not in never falling, but in getting up every time we do."

"I'm already up," I replied.

Lu popped open his door and said, "I'm right behind you." He unloaded my clubs from the trunk of his car and was a little dismayed to see me strap them on my back for my ride home because if I'd been planning on returning I would've left them in the storage room. "You sure you don't want to leave those here?" he asked.

"Yeah, I'm sure."

He stared at me as he frowned. His loser's buzz was gone. "Alright, then," he said.

I replied, "Alright, then," and I really think Lu expected to see me in the morning.

It was Saturday afternoon and for the first time I felt like I was on summer vacation. I had money in my pocket, nothing on my schedule, the freedom of Mom and Alicia being miles away and best of all a guilt-free conscience. I should have been happy and would have been if I hadn't royally screwed things up with Mel.

When I got home I called Ed and asked if I could move into his guesthouse for the rest of the summer while I tried to find a boarding school that would accept me on such late notice. He laughed and replied, "Well what'd you fly all the way back there for in the first place then!"

"Unfinished business," I told him.

Ed chuckled the conspiratorial laugh of a man familiar with putting out fires on blazing bridges and replied, "You're welcome here anytime. Let me know if you need a ride."

"With any luck I'll have one," I said.

"I'll keep my fingers crossed," he answered. Then he said, "Good luck."

I ordered a pizza, watched movies late into the night then joyously slept undisturbed in my bedroom. In the morning I started to pack but realized I no longer wanted anything from that life so all I kept was my golf clubs. When it was time to leave my house I stood on the front steps an extra long time and looked up and down the block. There would be no returning and even though I had spent so much time fantasizing this escape, when the moment came I was frozen. I think I was giving Mom one last chance. I looked up and down the block over and over and waited for her to turn the corner onto our street and apologize and beg me not to leave. But I couldn't wait forever and there was no traffic in sight so I took that first step and the world kept spinning.

My first stop was Harmony's Rest. I wasn't scheduled to read but everyone was up for it so we took a few hours and finished *Going After Cacciato*. They loved it and were curious what I'd read next and it wasn't easy to break the news that I wasn't coming back. I explained I was moving to Aspen to live with my father, and it was so odd to hear myself say those words. The old folks were the first people I actually told and a hushed murmur rolled through the little gathering as if they already knew some kind of scandal was involved. The place was a hotbed for gossip.

Cliff stayed behind after everyone left. He'd been sitting next to me while I read and hadn't let go of my arm since I told them I was leaving. When the room quieted to stillness he said, "So you met your old man and now you're moving in with him, eh? Will you come back and visit or is this it for you?"

"I don't know Cliff. I'm kinda running away."

"It's that mother of yours isn't it?"

"What do you mean?"

"Phyllis will be happy for you," he said mostly to himself. "Send me a letter every once in a while okay? Just remember Phyllis'll be reading it to me so mind your P's and Q's. We can come up with a code later if we need to."

"I'm gonna miss you Cliff," I told him.

He squeezed my arm and said, "Today is a good day Gates."

I left the retirement home and trekked downtown past Alicia's office to the St. Julien Hotel, which was almost as expensive as the Little Nell. I charged it to Mom's credit card because F her. The hotel had a business center and I went online to check my email. Timmy Timmy Timmy had sent me a message with an attached JPEG of Mrs. Vanleer in the hotel's bath. Her legs were draped over the sides of the tub spread-eagle and she clutched one of her new breasts proudly and puckered her lips for the camera. 3T's wrote, *This oughta keep you out of the clink. The woman's got a fierce smout.* Then he went on to tell me he'd decided to quit modeling after his job in Houston. It was his parents' idea. They had flown to New York to surprise him and tell him they'd invested his money wisely and it was time to focus on college. He said he woke up the next morning without his stutter and added, *You'll have to hear it to believe it.*

There was too much ground to cover in an email with 3T's. He was my best friend and I had a lot of explaining to do, especially once he got my postcard, so rather than write back I decided to wait until we could talk. He had shed his OCD tic and I had shed my secrets; it was a conversation worth waiting for.

I sent Melanie an email telling her I was moving to Aspen to live with my father and I'd be at the St. Julien Hotel until noon on Monday if she wanted to say goodbye. I told her she had given me a million reasons to love her and I had given her a million reasons not to love me so I'd understand if she didn't make it. And in a Hail Mary act of desperation I told her if she wanted she could come too. Her parents had fallen off the deep end. Marty wasn't showing any signs of slowing down and Mrs. Vanleer was just getting started so running away might be a good idea.

■

So that's where I am right now, sitting in the lobby of the St. Julien, waiting. It's 11:55 and she hasn't shown up yet but there's still five minutes. All I've been doing since yesterday is writing this down. I'm sure whatever boarding school I apply to will want an essay so let this serve as my letter for admission. It's probably longer than most but if you're gonna take me as a student you might as well know the real me. I'm guessing my history as a gambling, drink-spiking, godmother-fucking son of a suicidal lesbian won't help but everyone deserves a second chance.

■

It's noon now and I'm looking toward the street through a revolving door and don't see Melanie. A bellhop pushing a baggage cart layered with bags walks in front of me and is followed by a large family from the Middle East. The mother and daughters are wearing scarves over their faces and the sons are walking close behind them. The father is chattering a foreign dialect into a headset and trailing the group with his arms out like he's herding them. I watch them go all the way to the elevator and it's not until they're all squeezed into one car that I look back toward the hotel's entrance and see Melanie. She's smiling and carrying a large duffel bag so I think I can finally stop writing. If you want to know what happens next let me into your school and I promise to tell you the truth.